Tonight We Improvise

A Drama in Three Acts

Luigi Pirandello

Revised and Rewritten by
Marta Abba

A SAMUEL FRENCH ACTING EDITION

SAMUELFRENCH.COM
SAMUELFRENCH-LONDON.CO.UK

To Marta Abba,
so it will not die.
L. P.

Whenever the play is produced, all programs, printing and advertising for the play must set forth the following notice immediately below the title of the play:

"By Luigi Pirandello. Translated from the Italian by Marta Abba."

TONIGHT WE IMPROVISE

CHARACTERS

DR. HINKFUSS
THE LEADING ACTOR—RICO VERRI
THE LEADING ACTRESS—MOMMINA
THE CHARACTER ACTOR—SAMPOGNETTA
THE CHARACTER ACTRESS—SIGNORA IGNAZIA
TOTINA
DORINA
NENE
POMARICI
SARELLI
MANGINI   *Five Air Force Officers*
POMETTI
NARDI
THE SECRETARY
TWO LITTLE GIRLS *
THREE GIRLS
THREE BLOND DANCERS
6 OR 8 CUSTOMERS
THE JOKING CUSTOMER
NIGHTCLUB SINGER
A GENTLEMAN FROM THE ORCHESTRA
A GENTLEMAN FROM THE BALCONY
A GENTLEMAN FROM A BOX
A VERY OLD GENTLEMAN FROM A BOX
AN OLD LADY   *In the audience*
HER HUSBAND
A YOUNG SPECTATOR NEARBY
A YOUNG SPECTATOR IN THE ORCHESTRA
POET FROM THE BALCONY

4 CHOIRBOYS *
4 YOUNG GIRLS *
JOSEPH—AN OLD MAN *
MARY *
SHEPHERD *
YOUNG SHEPHERD *
A GROUP OF PEASANTS *
MUSICIANS AND CHOIR
8 OR 9 MEN AND WOMEN *

} *Procession*

* Non-speaking

Tonight We Improvise

ACT ONE

The theatre is filled tonight with that particular audience that always appears at the premiere of any new play.

The announcements, in the papers and on posters, of the unusual event of an improvised *performance has given rise to a great deal of curiosity in everyone. Only the critics from the papers seem to show none. They already feel quite sure they can chalk it all up tomorrow as a fiasco. ("Good Lord, for sure a bit like* commedia dell'arte *turned upside down. But where now can you get actors who can improvise the way those possessed performers of the* commedia dell'arte *used to? It was a good deal easier then, anyhow, with the ancient plots, traditional masks, and a repertory which facilitated the work. One sees in their faces, instead, a certain irritation, since they have neither read in the announcements nor otherwise been able to learn the name of the author who tonight has given the actors and their director whatever scenario they are using. Lacking any clue to remind them of judgments they have already made, they are uneasy, afraid to jump at certain conclusions which could show a contradiction on their part. Punctually at the hour designated for the performance, the LIGHTS in the theatre go down and the FOOTLIGHTS on stage softly come up.*

The audience, unexpectedly plunged into darkness, is at first attentive. Then, not hearing the buzzer that usually announces the parting of the curtains, they begin to rustle about in their seats. And all the more because from the stage, through the closed CUR-

TAINS, *confused and excited voices are heard—as though the actors were protesting about something, and someone else, reprimanding them, was trying to restore order and silence the uproar.*

A GENTLEMAN FROM THE ORCHESTRA. (*Looks around and loudly asks.*) What's happening up there?

ANOTHER FROM THE BALCONY. Sounds like a fight.

A THIRD FROM A BOX. Maybe it's all part of the show.

(*Someone laughs.*)

A VERY OLD GENTLEMAN FROM A BOX. (*As though the uproar were a personal insult to his seriousness as play-goer.*) What kind of scandalous behaviour *is* this? When has one *ever* had to put up with anything like it?

AN OLD LADY. (*Leaping up from her seat in the last rows of the orchestra like a frightened hen.*) God help us, it isn't a fire, is it?

HER HUSBAND. (*Immediately grabbing hold of her.*) Are you crazy? Fire indeed! Sit down and be quiet.

A YOUNG SPECTATOR NEARBY. (*With a melancholy smile of supportation.*) Don't you say it even as a joke. Anyhow, lady, they'd have let the safety curtain down.

(*Finally the BUZZER is heard on Stage.*)

SOME OF THE AUDIENCE. Ah!—at last!

OTHERS. Sssshhhh! Be quiet.

(*But the CURTAINS do not part. The BUZZER instead is heard still again. To this, from the back of the theatre, the irritated voice of the director, DR. HINK-FUSS, is heard replying. He violently pulls open the door at the back and angrily hurries down the aisle that divides in two the rows of the orchestra.*)

DR. HINKFUSS. *Why* the *buzzer? Why* the *buzzer?* Who ordered it rung? I'll order it, I alone, when it's time to. (*These words are shouted by* DR. HINKFUSS *as he comes down the aisle and climbs the three steps that join stage to orchestra. Then, controlling his nervous trembling with admirable speed, he turns to the audience. In a frock coat, a little scroll of paper under one arm,* DR. HINKFUSS *is one of those unfortunate creatures whose fate it is to be a tiny man hardly five feet tall. He compensates for this, in his way, with a great bushy head of hair. First he glances at his little hands, so small they perhaps inspire disgust even in him, scrawny and with the fingers as white and hairy as maggots, and then without giving much weight to his words says.*) I am deeply grieved by the momentary confusion the audience must have noticed going on behind the curtains just now, and I must ask their indulgence—though perhaps after all I might be said to wish it all to be taken as a sort of involuntary prologue—

THE GENTLEMAN FROM THE ORCHESTRA. (*Delightedly interrupting.*) Ah, there! Didn't I say so myself?

DR. HINKFUSS. (*With cold severity.*) What is it that the gentleman wishes to observe?

THE GENTLEMAN FROM THE ORCHESTRA. Nothing at all. I'm just pleased with myself for having guessed the whole thing.

DR. HINKFUSS. For having guessed exactly what?

THE GENTLEMAN FROM THE ORCHESTRA. That those noises on stage were all part of the show.

DR. HINKFUSS. Ah, yes? Is that so? It seemed to you that it was all being done as a trick? The very evening when I propose to myself to play with all my cards on the table. You're fooling only yourself, my dear sir. I said *involuntary* prologue, and, I will add, perhaps not at all inappropriate to a spectacle as unusual as the one you are about to witness this evening. But I must ask the audience not to interrupt me. Here it is, ladies and gentlemen. (*He takes from under his arm the little paper scroll.*) I have in this scroll of a few pages all I need. Almost nothing. A tale, hardly more, here and there interspersed with a little dialogue by a writer unknown to you.

SEVERAL IN THE AUDIENCE. What's the name? Who is it?

SOMEONE IN THE BALCONY. Who is it?

DR. HINKFUSS. Please, please, ladies and gentlemen. It is not at all my habit to call my audiences to attention. I do indeed wish to answer for all I have done, but I shall not allow you to call me to account during the performance itself.

THE GENTLEMAN FROM THE ORCHESTRA. But you said it hadn't started yet.

DR. HINKFUSS. Ah, yes, it has. And the very person who has the least right of any to deny it is exactly you, my dear sir, who took the noises on stage a few minutes ago as the start of the show. If I am here before you, the performance has begun.

THE VERY OLD GENTLEMAN IN THE BOX. (*Clearing his throat.*) I thought you were out here to apologize for those scandalous noises. I'll have you know— I've not come here to listen to a lecture by you or anyone else.

DR. HINKFUSS. A lecture indeed! How dare you think I'm out here to make you listen to a lecture? And how dare you proclaim such lies here in front of everyone? (THE VERY OLD GENTLEMAN IN THE BOX, *highly indignant at this apostrophe, leaps to his feet and muttering to himself leaves his box.*) Oh, so you can get up and leave, can you? No one's stopping you, my dear sir! I am here before you, ladies and gentlemen, solely to prepare you for the—unusual in what you are this evening about to see. I think I deserve your attention. You wish to know the author of this little tale? I could easily tell you.

SEVERAL IN THE AUDIENCE. Tell us. Go ahead and tell us. Do.

DR. HINKFUSS. All right, I will. Pirandello!

(*Exclamations from the audience: "Uhhh—"*)

THE GENTLEMAN IN THE BALCONY. (*Loudly, over the exclamations.*) And who is *he?*

(*Many of those in the boxes and the orchestra break out laughing.*)

DR. HINKFUSS. (*Laughing a little himself.*) Yes, it's always him, the incorrigible man. But though he did get away with it with two of my esteemed colleagues, giving the first of them six characters lost and looking for an author—what a really wretched innovation of the stage *that* was, unsettling everyone!—and the next time cunningly writing a *commedia a chiave* at which my other colleague saw his production broken off by the audience up in arms, this time there's no danger of his doing any such thing. Rest assured. I have—*eliminated* him. His name doesn't figure even on the posters. But then it would hardly have been fair of me to have made him responsible ever so slightly for this evening's performance. The only individual responsible for this evening is myself. I have taken one of his stories, as I would have taken one by anyone else. I preferred to take one of his because, of all writers writing for the theatre, it is perhaps he alone who has shown himself fully aware of the fact that the work of a writer is *finished* the moment he has finished putting the last word down on paper. He is responsible for the work to readers, of course, and to book reviewers, but neither can, nor should be, to theatregoers and to drama critics, who pass judgment sitting in a theatre.

VOICES IN THE THEATRE. Ah, no? Oh, lovely!

DR. HINKFUSS. No, ladies and gentlemen. For in the theatre the work of the writer no longer exists!

THE GENTLEMAN IN THE BALCONY. What's left, then?

DR. HINKFUSS. The scenic creation. The scenic creation I myself make of it and which is entirely my own. I must again ask the audience not to interrupt me. And let me caution you now (though I can already see some of the critics laughing) that I am firmly convinced of this theory of mine. The critics are masters at not taking such ideas seriously, of continuing to upbraid—unjustly, I maintain—the *writer* for what goes on in a theatre, even when they are quite willing to concede that the writer can laugh at their reviews just as they now are laughing at me and my theory of the theatre. Laugh, that is—it must be understood—if the reviews are unfavorable. If they're not, it would hardly be fair—would it?—for the writer to take for himself praise that belongs to *me?* My theory is based on solid reasons. Here in my hands is the work of the writer. (*He again shows the audience the same little scroll.*) What do I *do* with it? I take it for the subject of my scenic creation and *use* it—in the very way I use the skill of the actors I have cast, to play their roles according to the interpretations I have made, and of the designer whom I commission to design the sets, and of the stagehands who put them up, and of the electricians who light them—all according to instructions, advice, and indications, that I myself have given them. In a different theatre, with different actors and different sets, with different directions and different lighting, you will surely grant me the scenic creation would certainly be—different. Is it not then obvious from this that what one judges sitting in the theatre is never the work the writer had in his head but this or that scenic creation that had been made of it, each one different from the other—many, where the writer is unique? To judge a text it is necessary to know it. And in the theatre, where performed by certain actors it is one thing and by others necessarily another, one cannot. The work could be unique only if it could give *itself*, no longer employing actors but rather its own characters that, by some miracle, had assumed flesh and voice. In that case, yes, it could be judged in the theatre. But is such a miracle ever possible? To this day no one has ever seen it happen. And so, ladies and gentlemen, it is that which the director, with more or less dedication, tries for each night with his actors. The only thing he *can* do. To remove from what I am saying every appearance of paradox, I ask you to consider the fact that a finished work of art is fixed forever in an immutable form. This immutable form represents the poet's release from the toil of creation, the perfect quiet attained after all the agitation such toil entails. Good. Does it seem to you, ladies and gentlemen, that there can still be life where nothing any longer moves? Where all reposes in perfect stillness? Life must obey two imperatives, which, one equipoised against the other, permit it neither perpetually to be still nor always to be in movement. If life were always in movement, it would never be still. If it everlastingly were still, it would never move again. And life must both move and be still.

But the poet deludes himself when he thinks he has found release and tranquility in his work of art fixing life forever in immutable form. He has only ceased to live his own labor. Complete peace, complete tranquility is had only at the price of life itself. And how many people there are who suffer from this miserable delusion—who believe themselves still alive, when in fact they are so far gone they can't even smell the stench of their own corpses. If a work of art survives, it is only because we can still lift it out of the rigidity of its own form and let it loose inside ourselves, with our own life endow it with life—differently at different times for each of us. A work of art has many lives, not one. As one can infer even from the continual discussions born from not wanting to believe that it is so, it is *we* who give this life. Thus it is impossible for the life I give to a work of art to be like the life someone else is giving it. I ask your indulgence, ladies and gentlemen, for the round about way I have had to take in order to come to this, the point I wished to come to.

Someone could ask me: "But who told you art must be life? Life, yes, must obey the two opposing imperatives you speak of, and just for that very reason is not art. Just as art is not life, exactly because it succeeds in freeing itself from these same imperatives and reposes forever in the immutability of its own form. Exactly because of this, art is the kingdom of perfected creation, where life is as it ought to be, in an infinitely various and continually changing state of becoming. Each of us is seeking to create himself and his own life with those very faculties of the spirit that the poet employs in creating his work of art, and in fact he who is best instructed in these things and best knows how to use them succeeds both in reaching a higher state of being and in making it endure more constantly. But it will never be a true creation, first of all because it is doomed to wither and perish with us, in time; secondly, because, moving towards an end to be arrived at, it will never be free; and lastly, because, exposed to all the unforeseen and unforeseeable circumstances, to all the obstacles that others throw up against it, it perpetually risks being opposed, deviated, deformed. Art vindicates life, in a certain sense, because its creation, insofar as it is true creation, is freedom from time and from circumstances and has no end but itself."

Ah, yes, ladies and gentlemen, I reply, that's exactly how it is. Many times, however, I have happened to consider with anguished dismay the eternity of a work of art as an unreachable divine solitude from which even the artist himself, as soon as he has created it, is excluded. Terrible in its changelessness is the attitude assumed by a statue; terrible, this eternal solitude of immutable forms cast outside time. Every sculptor, I do not know but I imagine, after having created a statue, if he truly thinks he has given it a life which stands forever outside of time, should believe that his statue, like a living thing, could change its position and walk and speak. But then it would stop being a statue. It would become a living person. But only on *this* condition, ladies and gentlemen, can that which art has fixed in the immutability of form be brought to life, and turn, and move—on the condition that this form receive its movement from us who are alive; a life various and diverse and momentary, whatever each of us is capable of embuing it with. Today let us willingly leave works of art in that divine solitude they have, outside time. The audience, after a day full of worries and difficulties, anxieties and ordeals of every sort, in the evening, in the theatre, wish to be amused.

THE GENTLEMAN FROM THE ORCHESTRA. Good God! With Pirandello?

(Laughter.)

DR. HINKFUSS. You don't have anything to worry about. Rest assured. (*He once more shows the audience the little scroll.*) *This* is Pirandello. A mere trifle. The rest I do myself. I myself, all alone. And let me confide to you that I have created for you a delightful spectacle indeed, if the sets and scenes turn out with the same attention in each detail, and if my actors respond in every way to the faith I have placed in them. But in any case I shall be here with you, ready to intervene whenever necessary to lead the play back if it goes astray ever so slightly, to supplement any faulty workmanship with clarifications and explanations. And that, I like to think, will make you find the novelty of this effort at improvisation even more amusing. I have divided the performance tonight into a great many short scenes with brief pauses between, often only a moment of darkness from which a new scene will unexpectedly arise on the stage or, yes, even among you. Yes, in the theatre I've purposely left empty a box that will later be used by the actors, and then all of you will participate in the action. You will also be allowed an intermission so that you can get up and go out—but not to catch your breath, let me warn you now. I have prepared a new surprise for you even in the lobby. One last and very brief word—so that you can orient yourselves at once. The action takes place in a city in the interior of Sicily. Passions there, as you must know, are very strong, smoulder a long time and then flare forth with great violence. Above all, the fiercest passion is jealousy. Our tale in fact tells of one of these cases of the worst sort of jealousy. Worst because irremediable. Irremediable because it is that of time past. And it takes place exactly in the family where it least should have. For among the almost monastic seclusion of the other families in the city, it is the only one that has opened its doors to foreigners. It is a family with an excess of hospitality, given almost as if on purpose to challenge the inevitable gossip and scandal the whole town will make of it. The LaCroce family is composed, as you will see, of the father, Signor Palmiro, a mining engineer, who because of his continual absent-minded whistling is called Sampognetta, the toy whistle, by everyone; of the mother, Signora Ignazia, who comes from Naples and is known in her present surroundings as "The General"; and of four pretty daughters, shapely and flirtatious, vivacious and passionate: Mommina, Totina, Dorina, and Nene. And now, with your permission. (*He claps his hands as a signal for the actors and, pulling back one of the curtains a little, yells backstage.*) The buzzer. (*The BUZZER is heard.*) I'm calling the actors out to introduce the characters. (*The* CURTAINS *part. Towards the front of the stage a green scrim or a thin green traveller is seen that can be parted in the middle.* DR. HINKFUSS *pulls back the scrim or traveller a little and calls.*) Please, Mr. ————. (*He pronounces the name of* THE LEADING ACTOR, *who will play the part of* RICO VERRI. *But* THE LEADING ACTOR, *though there behind the scrim or traveller, is unwilling to come out.*) Please come out here, Mr. ————. Surely you'll not keep up our little argument here in front of the audience.

THE LEADING ACTOR. (*Dressed as* RICO VERRI *in the uniform of an air force officer, he emerges from behind the scrim or traveller greatly excited.*) I shall, sir. And all the more if you now go so far, here in front of the audience, as to call me by my real name.

DR. HINKFUSS. Have I offended you?

THE LEADING ACTOR. Yes, and continue to, not realizing what you're doing—keeping me here to discuss the matter with you after you've already forced me against my will to come out on the stage.

DR. HINKFUSS. Who asked you to discuss it? *You're* the only one discussing it. I called you out here merely to do what you are supposed to.

THE LEADING ACTOR. And I'm ready to. As soon as the play starts. (*He withdraws, using the green curtain scornfully.*)

DR. HINKFUSS. (*With difficulty staying where he is.*) I wanted to introduce you—

THE LEADING ACTOR. (*Coming back out.*) Never, sir. You shall not introduce me to a public that already knows me. Don't think for a minute I'm some little puppet in your hands. I am not to be shown off to the audience like that box you left empty up there, or a chair put here rather than there, all for some special scenic effect.

DR. HINKFUSS. (*Muttering between his teeth.*) You are at this moment profiting from the forbearance I must of necessity—

THE LEADING ACTOR. (*Quickly interrupting.*) No, my dear sir. No forbearance at all. You must remember that here, beneath these clothes, Mr. ———— (*He says his own name.*) no longer exists. He has given you his word to improvise this evening, and to do so, to have on his lips those lines that must rise from the depths of the character he represents, with the action that goes with them, with all the gestures completely natural, Mr. ———— must live the character of Rico Verri. And *is* already. So much so that, as I was just saying to you, I do not know how much longer I shall be able to endure all these accidents and surprises, these little games of light and shade you've prepared in order to amuse the audience. Do you understand?

(*There is heard at this point the reverberating whack of a slap, delivered behind the curtain, and immediately afterwards, the protests of* THE CHARACTER ACTOR, *who will play the part of* SAMPOGNETTA.)

THE CHARACTER ACTOR. O un! How do you like that? By God I didn't expect you to really hit me.

(*The protest is received with laughter behind the green curtain.*)

Dr. Hinkfuss. (*Peering through the green curtain.*) What the devil's happening now? Can something else be wrong?

The Character Actor. (*Coming out from behind the green curtain, his hand still nursing his cheek. Dressed up as* Sampognetta.) Just this—that I will not stand for Miss ————— (*The name of* The Character Actress.) with the mere excuse she's *improvising* to haul off and slap me so hard. You must have heard it. It has among other things—(*He unveils his cheek.*) ruined my makeup.

The Character Actress. (*Coming out dressed and made up as* Signora Ignazia.) Good heavens. Why not withdraw and try not to get hit by me? My slap was just a perfectly instinctive gesture.

The Character Actor. And how do I shelter myself from you if you hit me suddenly and without notice?

The Character Actress. Whenever you deserve it, dear.

The Character Actor. All right, but I have no way of knowing when I'm going to deserve it.

The Character Actress. Then you'll always have to be on guard because you're going to always be in need of a good whack or two. And, if one is really improvising, I cannot after all slap you at some moment decided on in advance.

The Character Actor. But there's no need to really hit me!

The Character Actress. And just what should I do then? *Pretend* to hit you? I haven't a written part to play. My lines come from here (*She makes a gesture from the stomach up.*) and I do not stand on ceremony, understand? You'll grab at me, and I'll let you have it.

Dr. Hinkfuss. Ladies and gentlemen, ladies and gentlemen, not here in front of the audience, please.

The Character Actress. We're already in our parts, Dr. Hinkfuss.

The Character Actor. (*Putting his hand again to his cheek.*) You said it!

Dr. Hinkfuss. So that's how it is, is it?

THE CHARACTER ACTRESS. Excuse me, but I thought *you* wanted to introduce us. Here we are introducing ourselves. One slap and this imbecile of a husband is good and introduced. (THE CHARACTER ACTOR, *as* SAMPOGNETTA, *starts whistling*.) There, see? He's whistling. Perfectly in character.

DR. HINKFUSS. But does it seem possible to you to have it done this way? In a chaos before the curtain and outside of the scenery?

THE CHARACTER ACTRESS. It does not matter. It does not matter.

DR. HINKFUSS. What do you mean it does not matter? Just what do you expect the audience to think?

THE LEADING ACTOR. They'll get it. They'll get it all the better this way. Leave it all up to us. We're all in character already.

THE CHARACTER ACTRESS. Everything will seem—you must believe it—much easier and more natural this way. None of the problems and restraints of a set place and action. We'll not forget to do everything you've planned for this evening. But just now, with your permission, I'm going to introduce my daughters. (*She pulls back the green curtain and calls*.) Come here, girls! Girls, come here! (*She takes the* FIRST *by the arm and pulls her out on the stage*.) Mommina. (*And then the* SECOND.) Totina. (*And then the* THIRD.) Dorina. (*And then the* FOURTH.) Nene. (ALL *except the* FIRST *make a graceful curtsey*.) Tocchi di ragazze! Thank God—all *four* of them deserve to be queens! Who'll ever guess they had *him* for a father? (THE CHARACTER ACTOR, *seeing that he is being pointed out, immediately averts his face and starts whistling*.) Whistle! Yes, go ahead and whistle. All you need in that sulphur mine of yours is for a little gas to get in your nose—just the way I might take a little pinch of snuff—and there you are, stretched out cold. And in one fine moment right before my eyes you're taken from me forever.

TOTINA. (*Running with* DORINA *to stop her*.) Please, Mama, please, don't start that.

DORINA. (*At the same time.*) Let it pass, Mama, please.

THE CHARACTER ACTRESS. Just look at him whistle, look at him! (*Then, coming out of character, to* DR. HINKFUSS.) Everything's going like clockwork, isn't it?

DR. HINKFUSS. (*With a wicked little gleam in his eye, finding here a way to get out of his predicament and save his battered prestige.*) As the audience must already have guessed, this rebellion against my orders among the actors was faked, agreed on in advance between them and me, in order to make the performance seem more authentic. (*At this underhanded getaway, the* ACTORS *stop and stare at him suddenly, like so many mannequins, in various poses of astonishment.* DR. HINKFUSS *notices it at once. He turns and looks at them and then points them out to the audience.*) Faked, too, this astonishment.

THE LEADING ACTOR. (*Trembling with indignation.*) A dirty trick! The audience must not believe a word of it. My protest was not in any way faked. (*He pushes back the green curtain as at first and strides off angrily.*)

DR. HINKFUSS. (*At once, confidently to the audience.*) Acting, acting, all acting, even this outburst. I should perhaps, after all, have conceded something to the ego of an actor like Mr. ————, indeed one of the very best on the stage today. But you surely understand that whatever happens here on this stage cannot be other than faked. (*Turning to* THE CHARACTER ACTRESS.) Yes, go on, go on, Miss ————, it is indeed going splendidly. But I could hardly have expected less from you.

THE CHARACTER ACTRESS. (*Disconcerted, dumbfounded by such impudence, not knowing any longer what to do.*) So, you want—you want me to go on? And—and —excuse me, please—go on with exactly what?

DR. HINKFUSS. Good God, with the performance, Miss ————,—it's off to such a splendid start, just as we planned it.

THE CHARACTER ACTRESS. No, listen, please. Don't say "just as we planned it" if you don't want me to stand here not able to say one single word.

DR. HINKFUSS. (*Again to the audience, as though in confidence.*) Marvelous. She's marvelous!

THE CHARACTER ACTRESS. You really want to make people believe that this emergence of our roles was agreed on between us ahead of time?

DR. HINKFUSS. Just ask the audience if they think we are not at this moment really improvising?

(THE GENTLEMAN IN THE ORCHESTRA, FOUR OTHERS IN THE ORCHESTRA, *and* THE GENTLEMAN IN THE BALCONY *start applauding. They stop at once if the real audience does not contagiously follow their example.*)

THE CHARACTER ACTRESS. But yes, of course, we are really improvising now. We're out of our roles and we're improvising, I as much as you.

DR. HINKFUSS. All right, then—keep it up, keep it up. Call the other actors out and introduce them.

THE CHARACTER ACTRESS. Right away. (*Calling behind the green curtain.*) All right, boys, all of you come out here! Don't worry, Dr. Hinkfuss, I'm in character! Out here, my friends!

(*Five young* AIR FORCE OFFICERS *enter noisily, in uniform. First they vigorously salute* SIGNORA IGNAZIA.)

THE FIVE OFFICERS. Cara Signora! Long live the General! Santa Pretettrice! (*And other similar exclamations. Then they greet* THE FOUR GIRLS, *who gaily reply.* ONE OF THE OFFICERS *goes over and also greets* SAMPOGNETTA. SIGNORA IGNAZIA *tries to interrupt all the uproar, indeed this time actually improvised.*)

SIGNORA IGNAZIA. Quiet, quiet, my dears. Let's not make too much noise. Wait, wait. Here, Pomerici, you're just what I've always dreamed of for my little Totina. Here, take her by the arm—like this! And you, Sarelli, you over here with Dorina.

THE THIRD OFFICER. Look here, Dorina's mine. (*Holding her by the arm.*) Let's not joke about it.

SARELLI. (*Pulling* DORINA *by her other arm.*) Come on, lay off. Let me have her. If her mother says she's mine, she's mine.

THE THIRD OFFICER. Not at all. We have an understanding, the signorina and I.

SARELLI. (*To* DORINA.) So, you have an understanding, do you? Congratulations! (*Denouncing them.*) Signora Ignazia, do you hear that?

THE CHARACTER ACTRESS. Understanding?

DORINA. (*Irritated.*) But of course, Miss ———— (*The name of* THE CHARACTER ACTRESS.) An *understanding*—about the *roles* we're playing.

THE THIRD OFFICER. I have to ask you, Miss ———— (*The name of* THE CHARACTER ACTRESS.), not to interfere with what's already been decided on.

THE CHARACTER ACTRESS. Oh dear. I'm sorry. Excuse me. Now I do remember. You, Sarelli, are with Nene.

NENE. (*To* SARELLI, *taking his arm.*) With *me!* Don't you remember that that's how we planned it?

SARELLI. Anyhow, we are here only to make noise.

DR. HINKFUSS. (*To* THE CHARACTER ACTRESS.) Attention, attention, Miss ————. I beg of you.

THE CHARACTER ACTRESS. Yes, yes. I'm terribly sorry. With so many of them I get all mixed up. (*Turning around to look.*) But Verri? Where is Verri? He ought to be here with his friends.

THE LEADING ACTOR. (*At once sticking his head out between the green curtain.*) Fine friends they are, giving your daughters here lessons in—modesty.

SIGNORA IGNAZIA. What do you want them to do? Treat them like nuns and teach them to embroider? Don't be old-fashioned, my dear. (*She goes and drags him out by the hand.*) Come now, be a sport. Come out here. Look at them. They're not a bit conceited and they have virtues, too. That can be said of very few girls now-a-days. All the virtues of good little wives—you who talks about modesty. Mommina is wonderful in the kitchen.

MOMMINA. (*Reproachfully, as though her* MOTHER *had betrayed a shameful secret.*) Mama!

SIGNORA IGNAZIA. Totina can patch and mend—

TOTINA. (*As* MOMMINA.) But what are you saying, Mama?

SIGNORA IGNAZIA. And Nene—

NENE. (*Quickly, aggressively threatening to clamp her hand on her* MOTHER'S *mouth*.) Mama, are you going to be still?

SIGNORA IGNAZIA. Find me anyone to equal the way she can take any old dress and make it over as good as new—

NENE. (*As before*.) Really, Mama, that's quite enough!

SIGNORA IGNAZIA. Get the spots out—

NENE. (*Clamping her hand on her* MOTHER'S *mouth*.) I said that was enough, Mama.

SIGNORA IGNAZIA. (*Pulling* NENE'S *hand away*.) Turning collars—and Dorina takes care of the accounts!

DORINA. *Now* have you scraped bottom?

SIGNORA IGNAZIA. What have things come to? They're *ashamed* of it.

SAMPOGNETTA. Just as if they were secret vices!

SIGNORA IGNAZIA. And they aren't vain, either. They're happy with so very little. Just so long as they get to the theatre now and then, they're willing to go hungry. Our old opera, that is. Even I like it a great deal.

NENE. (*Who comes in with a rose in her hand*.) But, Mama, don't forget *Carmen*, too. (*She puts the rose between her teeth and sings, wiggling her hips impudently*.)
"E l'amore uno strano augello
che non si puo domesticar—"

SIGNORA IGNAZIA. *Carmen's* all right, too, but it doesn't start your heart pounding the way our old opera does. Innocence cries out and no one believes her. And then, the lover in despair, "Ah! quell' infame l'onore ha venduto." Get Mommina to speak about all this. Basta! (*Turning around to* VERRI.) The first time you came to our house, remember?—you were introduced by these boys here—

THE THIRD OFFICER. If only we'd never done it—

THE SECOND OFFICER. He was an officer at our airfield—

THE LEADING ACTOR. Please, merely a reserve officer, for only six months and then, done with God willing, and done with *their* good times, too, enjoying life at my expense.

POMERICI. Us? At your expense?

SARELLI. Now listen here—

SIGNORA IGNAZIA. This is not the question. What I wanted to say was that neither I, nor my daughters here, nor their father over there— (*Again* SAMPOGNETTA, *the moment he is mentioned, turns his face and starts whistling.*) Stop it, or I'll smack you in the face with this purse. (*It is a large purse.* SAMPOGNETTA *stops at once.*) Not one of us had the least idea at the start that you had that damned Sicilian blood in your veins—

VERRI. I'm proud of it!

SIGNORA IGNAZIA. Ah! How I know it. God, how I know it!

DR. HINKFUSS. Please, please, Miss ———— (*He pronounces* THE CHARACTER ACTRESS' *name.*) Let's not give the plot away.

THE CHARACTER ACTRESS. No, don't worry, I won't.

DR. HINKFUSS. Only the introduction, clear and simple. That's all we want just now.

THE CHARACTER ACTRESS. Clear and simple, yes, don't you worry. But as I was saying, at first he didn't boast about it. Like the rest of us, he looked down on all those savages in town who thought it was shameful, our living *alla continentale,* our having in a few of the officers from the field and letting them have fun the way, my God, the way young people should, without anything shameful about it. And he had fun too, with my Mommina— (*She looks around her.*) Where is she? There she is. Come here, come over here, my poor girl. It's not time for you to stand there like that. (THE LEADING ACTRESS, *who will play* MOMMINA'S *part, is pulled by the hand, but pulls back.*) Come. Come along.

THE LEADING ACTRESS. Let me alone, Miss ————. *Please* let me alone. (*She pronounces the name of* THE CHARACTER ACTRESS. *Then resolutely she turns and faces*

Dr. Hinkfuss.) Dr. Hinkfuss, I simply cannot do it this way. I told you so right from the start. It simply is not possible for me. You sketched out the action for us and gave us the sequence of all scenes. All right. Then it should be that way. I'm supposed to sing. I must feel secure, in my place, in the action I've been assigned. I simply can't change every five minutes.

The Leading Actor. And why not? Possibly because Miss ———— (*He pronounces* The Leading Actress' *name.*) has already written down the lines she wants to say and memorized them.

The Leading Actress. I am prepared. Of course I am. And you perhaps are not?

The Leading Actor. Yes, but not with the very lines I'm going to say. Let's get this straight now. You are trying, aren't you, to get me to say certain things so you can use lines you've already prepared? I shall say what I feel like saying myself. (*An outburst of simultaneous comments from the* Actors *follows this argument.*) "That would be fine, wouldn't it?" "To have one get the other to say what suits *him!*" "There goes our improvisation!" "She might as well sit down and write out everybody's part!"

Dr. Hinkfuss. (*Cutting short the uproar.*) Ladies and gentlemen, please. I have already told you to say as little as possible, as little as possible. Enough for now. Introductions are over. What we need is more action and fewer words. You must pay attention to me. I assure you that your lines will come all by themselves, spontaneously, if you go through the action I've worked out for you. Do this and you can't go wrong. Let yourselves be guided by me, just the way we agreed on. Come now. Off stage. Let's have the curtain dropped. (*The stage* Curtain *is closed.* Dr. Hinkfuss, *remaining before the footlights and turning to the audience, adds.*) I must apologize, ladies and gentlemen. The performance is really ready to begin. Five minutes, just five minutes, with your kind permission, while I go and see that everything is ready. (*He withdraws, pushing aside the stage* Curtain. *A five-minute pause.*)

ACT TWO

The stage CURTAIN *again opens. But* DR. HINKFUSS *continues to put the audience off. It has occurred to him that it would be a good idea to start off with a religious procession, thereby giving the audience some Sicilian atmosphere. "It will add a little color," he says to himself. And he has seen to everything. For now just such a procession moves from the entrance of the theatre towards the stage, down the aisle that divides in two the rows of the orchestra. They enter in this order:*

1. FOUR CHOIRBOYS, *in black tunics and white shirts trimmed in lace, two before and two after, each bearing a lit taper in his hand;*

2. FOUR YOUNG GIRLS, *the "little virgins," dressed all in white and swathed in white veils, with white crocheted gloves so large their little hands seem clumsy in them—two before and two after. And each bearing one of the four supports of a little baldachin of skyblue silk;*

3. Under the baldachin, the Holy Family, consisting of AN OLD MAN *dressed like the St. Joseph one sees in holy pictures of the nativity, a purple halo on his head and on one hand a long staff, flowered at the crook; and beside him a beautiful blond young woman, with her eyes lowered, a modest smile on her lips, dressed like the* VIRGIN MARY. *She too has a halo on her head, and in her arms she carries a big beautiful wax doll, representing the Christ child, like the ones still seen today in crude Christmas pageants in Sicily; they are accompanied by* MUSICIANS *and* CHOIR;

4. A SHEPHERD *in a wool beret and coat, his trousers of goatskin, and* ANOTHER SHEPHPRD, *somewhat younger; one is playing the bagpipes and the other the flute;*

5. Bringing up the rear a GROUP OF PEASANTS of every age, the women in long skirts thickly pleated at the hips, veils on their heads, the men in short jackets and bell trousers, with wide belts of colored silk. In their hands are black cotton stocking caps with tassels on the ends. They come into the theatre singing, to the accompaniment of bagpipes:

> Oggi e sempre sia lodato
> nostro Dio sagramentato;
> e lodata sempre sia
> nostra vergine Maria.

6. DR. HINKFUSS, on the tail of the procession, watches the performance seated in the first row of the orchestra in a place reserved for him.

Meanwhile on stage one sees a street in the city. The rough white wall of a house runs from Left to Right across more than three quarters of the stage and then abruptly turns and runs upstage at an obtuse angle. At the corner, on a bracket attached to the wall, is a street light. Beyond the street light, in the wall, one sees the entrance to a night club, lit with colored lights, and, almost opposite but a little beyond and in relief, the portal of an old church with three steps leading up to it.

A little before the curtains are opened and the procession has entered the theatre, one hears on stage the sound of church bells and, hardly audible, the boom of an organ playing inside the church. When the CURTAINS part and while the procession is mounting the stage, there is seen along the wall and to the Right, MEN and WOMEN (not more than eight or nine) kneeling. These have just happened to be passing by. The WOMEN are crossing themselves; the MEN baring their heads. When, having crossed the stage, the PROCESSION has entered the church, these MEN and WOMEN join onto the end and enter, too.

When the last has gone in, the sound of the church bells stops. Now more clearly audible, the sound of the organ persists a moment longer in the silence, but it grows softer and softer and the lights dim out. Suddenly, the very moment the organ stops, there breaks out in shattering contrast the sound of a jazz band in the night club across the street; and at the same moment the white wall that runs across the stage becomes transparent. One sees the inside of the night club, glittering with colored lights. At the Right, near the entrance, is the bar, and, behind it, THREE GIRLS *in low cut dresses with too much make-up crudely smeared on their faces. Against the wall in back, next to the bar, a long drapery of flaming red velvet is hung, and, against it, composed like a basrelief, is a night club singer, dressed all in black gauze, her face pale, her head dropped to one side, her eyes closed. She is mournfully singing blues songs.* THREE BLOND DANCERS *move their arms and legs in rhythm and in unison turn their shoulders towards the bar. Only a small amount of space is left for them between the bar and the first row of small round tables. At the tables* A FEW CUSTOMERS *are seated with their drinks before them. Among the customers is* SAMPOGNETTA, *an old crumpled hat in his hand and a long cigar in his mouth.* A JOKING CUSTOMER *sitting behind him in the second row of tables, seeing him intently watching the movements of the* THREE BLOND DANCERS, *begins preparing a hideous joke: two long horns cut out of the light cardboard on which the wine list and program are printed.* THE OTHER CUSTOMERS *are quite aware of what he is doing and, delighted by the whole thing, urge him with winks and gestures to hurry. After the two horns are cut out, long and straight, from the circle of cardboard that forms their base,* THE JOKING CUSTOMER *gets up and with great caution places them on* SAMPOGNETTA'S *crumpled hat.* EVERYONE *starts laughing and applauding.* SAMPOGNETTA, *thinking the laughter and applause are for the* THREE BLOND DANCERS, *who have just finished their number, begins himself to laugh and applaud and, doing so, causes the others to laugh all the harder and applaud more noisily. He seems unable to understand why everyone is looking at him, including the* THREE GIRLS *at the bar. Even the* THREE BLOND DANCERS, *who have to exit, are laughing.* SAMPOGNETTA *is bewildered. He stops applauding. Then the strange* NIGHT CLUB SINGER, *overwhelmed with indignation, leaves her velvet backdrop and goes over and grabs the mocking trophy from* SAMPOGNETTA'S *head, crying.*

NIGHT CLUB SINGER. No, poor old man— (*To the* OTHERS.) Away, all of you. You ought to be ashamed! (THE CUSTOMERS *push her back, all crying out at once in great confusion.*)

THE CUSTOMERS. Stay out there, stupid! Shut up and get back where you belong. *Where's* the poor old man? Leave it alone! You keep out of this! He's got what he deserves! He deserves it!

NIGHT CLUB SINGER. (*Continues to protest and, restrained by the* OTHERS, *struggles to get free.*) You cowards, let go of me! Why does he deserve it? What has he done to you?

SAMPOGNETTA. (*More bewildered than ever, now stands up.*) I *deserve* what? What do I *deserve?*

THE JOKING CUSTOMER. Come on, why don't you get out of here? This is no place for you, sir! (*He, with the help of the* OTHERS, *pushes* SAMPOGNETTA *towards the door.*)

THIRD CUSTOMER. We know perfectly well what *you* deserve, Signor Palmiro!

(SAMPOGNETTA *is led out with the horns still on his head. The lights are extinguished behind the transparent wall, and it becomes a wall again. The cries of those trying to restrain the night club singer continue to be heard. Then a big burst of laughter and the jazz starts up again.*)

SAMPOGNETTA. (*To THE TWO or THREE CUSTOMERS who have pushed him out into the street and who now stand relishing the sight of him with his crown underneath the street light.*) What I'd like to know is what happened?

SECOND CUSTOMER. Nothing, really. It's all because of the little incident the other night.

THIRD CUSTOMER. Everyone knows you care about that night club singer—

SECOND CUSTOMER. Just for laughs they were hoping she would slap you as she did the other night—

THIRD CUSTOMER. Exactly—saying it was what you *deserved!*

SAMPOGNETTA. Ah, I understand now! I understand!

FIRST CUSTOMER. Look—hey, look up there in the sky, all of you. Stars!

SECOND CUSTOMER. Stars?

THIRD CUSTOMER. What are you talking about? *Stars?*

FIRST CUSTOMER. They're moving. They're moving.

SECOND CUSTOMER. Come on. Come on.

SAMPOGNETTA. Is it possible?

FIRST CUSTOMER. Yes, yes, just look. It's as though, with a couple of poles, you could reach right up and touch them. (*He raises his arms, making the shape of two horns.*)

THIRD CUSTOMER. You think those bulbs there are stars?

SECOND CUSTOMER. You were saying, Signor Palmiro—?

SAMPOGNETTA. Ah, yes, yes. I was trying to say that this evening, I don't know if you noticed it, I expressly kept my eyes fixed all the time on the little dancers, without once turning my head towards her. She makes such an impression on me, ah, such an impression, that poor soul, when she sings: her eyes closed and those tears streaming down her face!

SECOND CUSTOMER. That's an act, Signor Palmiro! Do not pay any attention to those tears. It's all part of the show.

SAMPOGNETTA. (*Seriously shaking his head and waving "no" with his finger.*) No, no, ah, no, no, not at all. An act indeed! That woman suffers. She really and truly suffers. And then her voice is the very voice of my eldest girl. Exactly. Exactly. And she's told me herself, in confidence of course, she too comes from a very good family—

THIRD CUSTOMER. Ah yea? Just listen. A daughter of some engineer perhaps—?

SAMPOGNETTA. That I wouldn't know. But I do know that misfortunes can befall anyone. And every time I hear her sing, I become grieved and dismayed—

(*At this point enter from the Left, marching,* TOTINA *on* POMARICI'S *arm,* NENE *on* SARELLI'S, DORINA *on that of* THE THIRD OFFICER, MOMMINA *at* RICO VERRI'S *side, and* SIGNORA IGNAZIA *on the arm of* THE OTHER TWO OFFICERS. POMARICI *is beating out the time for all of them, even before they come on stage.* THE THREE CUSTOMERS, *who have now become a group of four or more, hearing a voice, withdraw towards the entrance to the night club, leaving* SAMPOGNETTA *alone under the street light. The horns are still on his head.*)

POMARICI. One—two, one—two, one—two—

(*They march in, facing the audience. The* FOUR DAUGHTERS *and* SIGNORA IGNAZIA *are dressed up in gaudy evening dresses.*)

TOTINA. (*Seeing her father with horns on his head.*) Oh God, Papa—what have they done to you?

POMARICI. Those filthy cowards!

SAMPOGNETTA. To me? What are you talking about?

NENE. But take that thing off your head!

SIGNORA IGNAZIA. (*While her husband feels around his hat with his hands.*) Horns?

DORINA. Rascals—who did it?

TOTINA. Just look over there!

SAMPOGNETTA. (*Taking off the horns.*) On me—horns?
Ah then, it was *this* all along. Scoundrels.

SIGNORA IGNAZIA. And he's still holding them in his
hand. Throw them away, you idiot. All you're good for
is to be the butt of every rogue in town.

MOMMINA. (*To her* MOTHER.) That's all we need now,
for you to scold *him* for it—

TOTINA. —while those filthy cowards are to blame.

VERRI. (*Going towards the entrance to the night club.
To* THE CUSTOMERS *who have been standing by watching
and laughing.*) Which of you did it? Which of you did it?
(*He grabs one of them by the chest.*) You? Was it you?

NENE. They're *laughing!*

THE CUSTOMER. (*Trying to get free.*) Let go of me. I
had nothing to do with it. You better keep your hands
off me!

VERRI. Then tell me who did it.

POMARICI. Come on, Verri. Let's get out of here.

SARELLI. What's the point of remaining for a row?

SIGNORA IGNAZIA. No, no, no. I must have an apology,
a personal apology, from the proprietor of this—den of
iniquity.

TOTINA. Let's go, Mama, please.

SECOND CUSTOMER. Careful how you speak there, Signora. There are also gentlemen around here.

MOMMINA. Do gentlemen behave this way?

DORINA. You filthy fools!

THIRD OFFICER. Let's go, Signorina, let's go.

FOURTH CUSTOMER. Just the boys, playing a little
joke—

POMARICI. So you call it a joke, do you?

SECOND CUSTOMER. We all have the highest regard for
Signor Palmiro here—

THIRD CUSTOMER. (*To* SIGNORA IGNAZIO.) But as for
you, Signora, not one damned bit!

SECOND CUSTOMER. Everyone in town's talking about
your behavior.

VERRI. (*Going towards him with raised arms.*) Watch out what you say there, or I'll knock you down.

FOURTH CUSTOMER. We'll report you to the Colonel.

THIRD CUSTOMER. Such conduct in an officer.

VERRI. Who'll report it?

THE CUSTOMERS. (*Also those inside the night club.*) All of us—we all will!

POMARICI. You started this. You insult the ladies walking down the street in our company, and it's our duty to defend them.

FOURTH CUSTOMER. No one insulted them!

THIRD CUSTOMER. No—it was the Signora who started insulting us!

SIGNORA IGNAZIA. I—never! I insulted no one. All I did was tell you to your dirty faces what you are—fools, imbeciles, rogues—that's what you are, and you ought to be under lock and key in cages, the way wild animals are. There. That's what I think of you. (ALL THE CUSTOMERS *laugh a little awkwardly.*) Go ahead. Laugh. Laugh, you scoundrels, savages.

POMARICI. (*With* THE OTHER OFFICERS *and* THE DAUGHTERS, *trying to calm her down.*) Come, come, Signora, let's go—

SARELLI. We've had enough of this.

THIRD OFFICER. Let's get on to the show.

NENE. Mama, don't you debase yourself by having anything more to do with them.

FOURTH OFFICER. Let's go. We're already late.

TOTINA. The first act'll be over, I'm sure.

MOMMINA. Yes, yes, let's go, Mama. Leave them to their dirty tricks.

POMARICI. Signor Palmiro, you come on to the theatre with us.

SIGNORA IGNAZIA. Him at the theatre? Oh, no! Get home! Get home this minute! You have to get up early tomorrow for the mine. Go on! Go home! (THE CUSTOMERS *turn and laugh at this peremptory order frc the wife to her husband.*)

SARELLI. And we must get to the theatre. Let's not lose any more time.

SIGNORA IGNAZIA. Imbeciles. Cretins. Go ahead and laugh. Laugh at your ignorance.

POMARICI. Enough of this now. Enough of this!

THE OTHER OFFICERS. Yes, let's get to the theatre, to the theatre.

DR. HINKFUSS. (*At this point he gets up and cries.*) Yes, quite enough, quite enough. Now off to the theatre! Everyone off stage. The customers get back in the night club and the rest of you exit right. And pull the curtains too, just a little, on both sides.

(THE ACTORS *exit. The stage curtain is pulled a little from either side so that there is left exposed in the Center the section of the white wall that will serve as the screen for the film about to be shown of the opera. Only* THE CHARACTER ACTOR (SAMPOGNETTA) *has stayed on the stage after the others have exited. If the theatre does not have boxes, at this point and during the next few speeches of* DR. HINKFUSS *and* THE CHARACTER ACTOR, *stage hands can bring on-stage a very simple box arrangement and set it up Downstage Right. They also bring on straight chairs and a bench and place them within the framework of the box, so that when* THE ACTORS *and* ACTRESSES *enter they will sit on an angle facing the screen— three quarters of each face towards the audience.*)

THE CHARACTER ACTOR. (*To* DR. HINKFUSS.) But if I'm not going to the theatre with them, I should go off Left, shouldn't I?

DR. HINKFUSS. What a question! Of course you should go off Left.

THE CHARACTER ACTOR. No, I wanted only you to consider, my dear director, that they didn't let me say a single word. Too much confusion!

DR. HINKFUSS. Not at all. It went—beautifully!! Go on, get off stage.

THE CHARACTER ACTOR. I have to clarify that it is *I* who always have to pay for everything.

DR. HINKFUSS. Very well. Now you have, and now you can get off the stage. We're going to have the theatre scene now. (THE CHARACTER ACTOR *exits Left*.) Is the turntable ready? And the projector? Start them up.

(DR. HINKFUSS *turns to sit down in his seat. Meanwhile, at the Right of the stage behind the stage curtain drawn to hide the corner edge where the wall bracket with the street light is, the stage hands have set up a phonograph on which they have put the end of the first act of an Italian opera, "La Forza del Destino" or "Un Ballo in Maschera" or some other. It is synchronized with the film being shown on the white wall that serves as a screen. The sound and the projection have barely begun, however, before the box that has been left empty, or the box set-up onstage, is lit up, with a strong light whose source one cannot see, and* SIGNORA IGNAZIA *is seen entering with her* FOUR DAUGHTERS, RICO VERRI, *and* THE OTHER OFFICERS. *Their entrance is noisy and immediately arouses protests from the audience.*)

SIGNORA IGNAZIA. Now see if I wasn't right! It's already the first act finale.

TOTINA. Ohhhh, how we've rushed! Auf. (*She sinks down in the first seat in the box, opposite her mother.*) God, it's hot here!

POMARICI. (*Making a fan of his cap.*) Here I am, Signorina, at your service!

DORINA. Of course! On close ranks! One—two, one—two—

VOICES IN THE THEATRE. But *really!* Silence! Is this any way to enter a theatre?

MOMMINA. (*To* TOTINA.) You've got my seat. Get up.

Totina. Well, if Dorina and Nene are sitting down in the middle—

Dorina. We thought Mommina would want to sit in back with Verri, like the other time—

Voices in the Theatre. Sssshhhhhh—quiet. Quiet. The same people again. It's simply indecent. And the really shocking thing is they're *officers!* Isn't there anyone here to make them be still?

(*Meanwhile there is great confusion in the box while everyone changes places.* Totina *gives up her place to* Mommina *and takes* Dorina's. Dorina *has moved over into the place left empty by* Nene, *who has gone over and sat on the divan next to her mother.* Rico Verri *sits next to* Mommina *on the divan opposite. Behind* Totina, Pomarici. *Behind* Dorina, The Third Officer. *And in back,* Sarelli *and* The Other Two Officers.)

Mommina. Gently, gently, for God's sake!

Nene. Yes, gently! First you cause all this mixup—

Mommina. I?

Nene. Yes, making everyone get up and change seats—

Dorina. *Let* them talk!

Totina. As if they'd never heard ————— (*She names the opera.*) before.

Pomarici. Still one ought to have a little respect for the ladies.

Voices in the Theatre. Shut up, you. It's simply shocking. Throw them out! Can it really be the box the officers are in that's making all the noise? Out! Out!

Signora Ignazia. Cannibals! Is it our fault if we happen to get here a little late? Do you call *this* civilization? First we're assaulted on the street, and now here in the theatre we're shouted at and insulted. Cannibals!

Totina. This is the way it's done on the continent!

Dorina. One comes to the theatre when one feels like it.

NENE. And with us are people who know how one lives and does things on the continent.

VOICES IN THE THEATRE. Enough. Enough.

DR. HINKFUSS. (*Getting up and turning to the box where the actors are.*) Yes, enough, enough. Let's not carry it too far, I beg of you.

SIGNORA IGNAZIA. But it pleases me to carry it this far. We're being egged on from down there. It is an absolutely insupportable persecution, don't you see? to have all these insults thrown at us just because we happen to make a bit of noise getting into our seats—

DR. HINKFUSS. All right. All right. This is enough for now. Anyhow the act's over.

VERRI. Over? Thank God. Let's get out then.

DR. HINKFUSS. Excellent. Yes, out, out!

TOTINA. I'm so thirsty. (*She leaves box.*)

NENE. Let us hope to find some ice cream.

SIGNORA IGNAZIA. Come, let's get out of here, or I'm going to blow up!

(*The film is done. The phonograph is silent. The* CUR-
TAIN *closes completely now.* DR. HINKFUSS *gets
up on the stage and turns to the audience as the
LIGHTS come on in the theatre.*)

DR. HINKFUSS. Those of the audience who usually go out between acts are free to do so now if they like. They can have a good look at the scandal that those dear people have aroused, even out in the lobby—not willfully but because by now everything they do is scrutinized and examined and becomes still something else for people to gossip about. Go on, then. But not everyone, please. I don't want it too crowded outside with everyone trying to see what more or less has already been seen in the box. I can assure you that whoever stays here in his seat will miss absolutely nothing of consequence. You will see, out there mixing with the audience during the usual intermission between acts, the same people you saw leave their box a moment ago. I myself, here in the theatre, shall profit from this interruption to change scenes, doing so right here in front of you, ladies and gentlemen, clearly in view, to offer you who are staying in your seats something a little out of the ordinary, too. (*He claps his hands as a signal and commands.*) Open the curtains!

(*The* CURTAINS *open.*)

INTERLUDE

Simultaneous performances in the lobby and on stage: In the lobby the ACTORS *and* ACTRESSES, *each of course still in his role, behave with complete freedom and naturalness, as though he was merely a part of the audience during intermission. They group themselves at four different places in the lobby and there, each group, independent from the other, performs a simultaneous scene:* NENE *and* TOTINA, *who go with* POMARICI *and* SARELLI *to the far end of the lobby where there is a counter at which coffee, beer, soft drinks, caramels, and other such things are sold;* DORINA *walks up and down as she talks with* THE THIRD OFFICER (NARDI); RICO VERRI *with* SIGNORA IGNAZIA, *sitting on a bench, with the* OTHER TWO OFFICERS (POMETTI *and* MANGINI) *and* MOMMINA. *These little scenes, though taking place simultaneously and in different parts of the lobby, are written here, because of space, one after the other.*

I

(NENE, TOTINA, POMARICI, *and* SARELLI *at the counter at the far end of the lobby.*)

NENE. What, you don't have any ice cream? Oh, what a shame. Give me a soft drink, then, but it *must* be cold. I insist. Yes, cherry's all right.

TOTINA. And lemonade for me.

POMARICI. And a little bag of chocolates, and some caramels, too.

NENE. No, don't get any caramels, Pomarici. Thank you.

TOTINA. They won't be any good. They are? Well, get

them, then, go ahead and get them. It's one of the nicest things in the world—

POMARICI. Caramels?

TOTINA. No—for us women—to make men pay for things.

POMARICI. It is such a little thing. I'm sorry we did not go to the drugstore before coming to the theatre—

SARELLI. With what has happened—?

TOTINA. Didn't you say he'd be on leave, the *beast,* and very soon?

NENE. I simply don't see why not. All I want to do really is fly over town just for the pleasure of leaning out and spitting on it. Can't I really, can't I?

SARELLI. Go up? It's absolutely out.

NENE. No, I mean spit—puh! like that, just once. Well, you'll have to do it for me, then.

II

(DORINA *and* NARDI, *the* THIRD OFFICER, *walking up and down.*)

NARDI. But didn't you know? Your father's simply crazy about that night club singer!

DORINA. Papa? What are you telling me?

NARDI. Papa. Papa. I'm telling you myself. And everyone in town knows all about it.

DORINA. You aren't serious. Papa in love? (*She bursts out laughing and all the audience turns to look at her.*)

NARDI. Didn't you *see* her over there in the night club?

DORINA. For God's sake, don't let Mama know about it. She'd skin him alive. But who is she? Do you know her?

NARDI. I've seen her once. Some crazy girl all broken up over something or other.

DORINA. Broken up? How?

NARDI. They say she always cries when she sings, with her eyes closed. Real tears. And sometimes she even faints and falls down on the floor, from whatever it is that makes her cry so. Drunk.

TOTINA. Good lord. Even if he is my father I must say he does go out of his way looking for trouble, going to places like that.

POMARICI. (*Putting a chocolate in her mouth.*) Don't you worry about it. Don't worry about it.

NENE. (*Opening her mouth like a little bird.*) Don't I get one, too?

POMARICI. (*Putting one in her mouth too.*) There you are, baby, but you get a caramel instead.

NENE. Are you sure this is the way people on the continent behave?

POMARICI. What do you mean? Feed the pretty girls candy? Absolutely.

SARELLI. That, and a good deal more, too.

NENE. What else? What else?

POMARICI. Oh, if you only wanted to do *everything* just the way we do it on the continent.

TOTINA. (*Provocative.*) What, for example?

SARELLI. Can't show you here.

NENE. And then tomorrow the four of us are storming the airfield—

TOTINA. And if you don't take us up for a ride, we'll never have anything more to do with you.

POMARICI. We'll love seeing you, but as for going up to fly with us, well—

SARELLI. Against regulations!

POMARICI. With that commander we have in charge out there—

DORINA. Oh? Then it's being drunk that does it.

NARDI. Maybe. Or maybe she drinks because she's so miserable.

DORINA. Oh God, and Papa—? Poor dear. But does he know everyone's talking about him? No, no, I don't believe it.

NARDI. You don't believe it? Even if I told you that one night—maybe he was a little high, too—he made a fool of himself in front of everyone in the night club, getting up and going over—with tears in his eyes, too, and a handkerchief in his hand—to dry her tears, while she stood there singing with her eyes closed?

DORINA. But, no—you aren't serious!

NARDI. And you know what she did? She let go with a terrific slap!

DORINA. She slapped Papa? She, too? Poor Papa. Mama gives him enough as it is.

NARDI. That's what he said himself, right there before everyone, with all of them laughing. "You do it, too, you ungrateful girl. My wife gives me plenty of them as it is."

(*By now they are near the counter.* DORINA *sees her sisters,* TOTINA *and* NENE, *and with* NARDI *she rushes towards them.*)

III

(*In front of the counter:* NENE, TOTINA, DORINA, POMARICI, SARELLI, *and* NARDI.)

DORINA. Can you imagine what Nardi's been telling me? Papa's in love. With that night club singer.

TOTINA. No!

NENE. Do you believe it? It's just a joke.

DORINA. No, no, it's *true*. It's true.

NARDI. I can prove it's true.

SARELLI. Sure. I knew it all along.

DORINA. And if you only knew what he did—

NENE. What?

DORINA. He got slapped by her, too, right in front of everyone, in the night club.

NENE. Slapped?

TOTINA. But why?

DORINA. He wanted to dry her tears.

TOTINA. Her tears?

DORINA. Yes, you see, they say she's a girl who's always crying—

TOTINA. There. Wasn't I right when I said it just now?

It's he who causes it all. What can you expect? Why shouldn't people laugh at him?

SARELLI. If you want proof, just reach in the inside pocket of his coat. He ought to have the picture of the singer tucked away there. He showed it to me the other day, with tears and comments. Poor Signor Palmiro

IV

(RICO VERRI *and* MOMMINA, *apart from the others.*)

MOMMINA. (*A little frightened by the gloomy look with which* VERRI *came out of theatre box.*) What's the matter?

VERRI. (*Hiding awkwardly his annoyance.*) Me? Nothing. What do you mean, "What's the matter?"

MOMMINA. But then why are you acting like this?

VERRI. I don't know. All I know is that if I'd been cooped up in that box one more minute, I'd have committed a crime for sure.

MOMMINA. I can't bear such a life any longer!

VERRI. (*Loudly and angrily.*) Have you noticed it just now?

MOMMINA. Please, please, don't speak so loudly. Everyone's looking at us.

VERRI. That's what I say. That's exactly what I say.

MOMMINA. I've gotten to the point I hardly dare raise my hand or say a single word.

VERRI. What I'd like to know is what business they have looking at us like that, standing here listening to every word you and I say to each other.

MOMMINA. Please, be good and do me this one favor— don't provoke them.

VERRI. Aren't we here like everyone else? What's so funny about us at this moment that they just stand and stare at us? I ask you, is it possible—

MOMMINA. Yes—to really live—I've already told you —to even make a single gesture any more, raise one's eyes even, when everyone's always staring. Look over there, around my sisters, and over there around Mama.

VERRI. Just as if we were here giving a performance in a play.

MOMMINA. Exactly.

VERRI. Unfortunately, your sisters over there—I am sorry to say—

MOMMINA. What?

VERRI. Nothing. I'd rather not pay any attention to it. But it seems to me they rather enjoy—

MOMMINA. Enjoy what?

VERRI. Being stared at.

MOMMINA. But they aren't doing anything wrong. They're laughing and talking—that's all.

VERRI. It's a challenge. That bold behaviour!

MOMMINA. But *your* friends are to blame—

VERRI. I know. To lead them on. Believe me, they're beginning to get in my hair—Sarelli there, and Pomarici, and Nardi.

MOMMINA. They're simply having a little fun.

VERRI. Fun? At the expense of the reputations of three young women. They could at least keep from doing certain things, certain little familiarities here in public—

MOMMINA. Yes, you're right, about that.

VERRI. I, for example, would no longer tolerate one of them permitting himself with you—

MOMMINA. First of all, I would not allow it. You know that.

VERRI. Let me go on, please. Even you, even you at first let them.

MOMMINA. But not any more, not for a long time. You know that.

VERRI. It isn't that I know it. They must know it, too.

MOMMINA. They do. They do.

VERRI. They do not. More than once they've tried to show me they don't—just to prove to me they can.

MOMMINA. Not at all. When? Please, please. Don't get such ideas—

VERRI. They ought to know they can't joke with me about these things.

MOMMINA. They do—you can be sure of that. But the more you let on how it upsets you, even as a joke, the more they'll try and do it, just to show you they weren't malicious about it in the first place.

VERRI. So then, you forgive them?

MOMMINA. No, it isn't that at all. I'm saying all this just for you, so you won't be so upset. And for myself, too. Knowing how you feel, I live in a continual state of trepidation. Let's go now. Let's go. Mama just motioned to me. I think she's ready to go back in.

V

(SIGNORA IGNAZIA, *sitting on a bench, with* POMETTI *and* MANGINI, *flanking her.*)

SIGNORA IGNAZIA. Ah, boys, you could acquire many merits in the eyes of—civilization.

MANGINI. Us? How, Signora?

SIGNORA IGNAZIA. How? Why in giving a few lessons at your club.

POMETTI. Lessons, Signora? To whom?

SIGNORA IGNAZIA. To these rude, uncouth, boorish villagers. If only an hour a day.

MANGINI. Lessons in what?

POMETTI. In manners?

SIGNORA IGNAZIA. No, no, no, in behavior. In how it's done. In comme il faut. One little lesson a day, one hour a day, just to show them how one really lives outside this island in great cities. You—where do you come from, my dear Mangini?

MANGINI. I? From Venice, Signora.

SIGNORA IGNAZIA. Venice. God, Venice—the city of my dreams. And you, you, Pometti?

POMETTI. From Milan.

SIGNORA IGNAZIA. Ah, Milan. Milano. Think of it. El nost Milan—I myself come from Naples, from Naples,

which is—I don't want to insult Milan, but I must say it
—and fully granting the charms of Venice—is, is, in its
very essence a paradise. Chiaia. Posillipo. I can't help it.
I simply can't help crying every time I think of Napoli.
The things there are there, the things. Oh, that Vesuvius.
And Capri. You, you of course have the Duomo, and the
Galleria, and La Scala. And you, ah, the Piazza San
Marco, the Grand Canal. Such things they are! While
here, all these *"fetenzierie!"* They stink! And would this
be seen only outside in the streets!

MANGINI. Don't say it to their faces so loudly, please,
Signora.

SIGNORA IGNAZIA. No, no, I want to speak loudly. Fetenzierie! They have it in their blood, in their very bones.
Always growling about something. Isn't that the impression you get? That they're ready to slit your throat at
the drop of a pin?

MANGINI. Really, as far as I personally am con-
cerned—

SIGNORA IGNAZIA. Come, come, doesn't it seem so to
you? Of course it does. They're all burning up with a—
what shall we call it? Yes, with a rage they must have
been born with, that makes them turn on each other like
wild animals. All you have to do—I don't know—is look
here instead of there, or blow your nose a little hard, or
smile from something you are thinking. God save us!
"He's laughing at me! He blew his nose like that just
as an affront! He looked around like that just to insult
me!" You can't do anything without their thinking there's
an insult intended. Just because, all of them, have the
very devil down inside them. Just look in their eyes. It
scares the breath straight out of you. The eyes of
wolves—! *Su. Su. Su.* Let's get up. It's time to go back
in. Let's go and rescue those poor girls.

(*The time each of the four groups need for saying its
    lines, each in its designated place in the lobby, has
    been measured. Lines have been cut or added where
    necessary so that all four groups finish at the same*

time and simultaneously start towards each other in leaving the lobby. This interlude must also be synchronized with the time needed for DR. HINKFUSS *onstage to perform the scenic miracles he has planned. Such miracles could simply be left up to* DR. HINKFUSS' *bizarre powers of invention, but since it was he himself, and not the author of the short story, who chose to make* RICO VERRI *and the other* OFFICERS *aviators, it seems likely he did so in order to have the pleasure at this point of preparing for the public left in the theatre the beautiful scenic effects of an airfield at night, under a magnificent starry sky. Everything on the ground is small, to give the impression of infinite space bounded only by starstrewn sky; in back, the white buildings that house the* OFFICERS, *with their small lit windows, here and there scattered about the field two or three airplanes, all very small. One hears the roar of an airplane out of sight, flying in the tranquil night.*

We shall let DR. HINKFUSS *take the pleasure of producing all this even if not a single member of the audience remains in the theatre. In this case, which of course one must be prepared for, the simultaneous performances both in the lobby and onstage do not of course take place.* DR. HINKFUSS *orders the curtains opened, but, seeing that he is unable to keep even a small part of the audience in the theatre, he retires into the wings, somewhat annoyed, to give proof of his scenic bravura only when the performances in the lobby are over and the audience, recalled by the buzzer, have come back into the theatre and taken their seats again.*

What is important is that the audience be made to see things that, if not exactly superfluous, are certainly quite peripheral. But granted that one can see, by many different signs, that the audience takes great delight in all this and goes after it more greedily than simpler fare, still DR. HINKFUSS *should put it to good use.* DR. HINKFUSS *says clearly and with the disdain of a great lord who permits himself certain extravagances, "The airfield scene could be omitted since it is not, strictly speaking, necessary. But, although a little time will be lost in creating a certain beautiful effect, you will understand that one does not want to lose time so another scene will be skipped that can easily be omitted without damage to our play." We, for our part, shall omit the directions DR. HINKFUSS can readily think up for himself, to the scene changers and electricians and stagehands, for the setting up of the airfield. Barely done, he gets down off the stage and into the orchestra, plants himself firmly in the middle of the aisle to direct with still other appropriate commands the lighting effects. And when he has them just right, he goes back onstage.)*

DR. HINKFUSS. No! no! no! Clear everything! Clear everything! Stop the motor of the airplane. Turn the lights off. I'm thinking that we can do better without this scene. Yes, the effect we have is very pretty, but, with the means we have at our disposal, we can get other effects no less pretty that further the action even more effectively. Luckily this evening I am quite frank with you, ladies and gentlemen, completely honest with you, and I trust it will not displease you to see just how one puts a show on, not only under your very eyes but even (and indeed why not?) with your collaboration. You see, ladies and gentlemen, the theatre is the yawning mouth of a gigantic machine that is—hungry: a hunger, I should add, that these gentlemen the poets—

A POET FROM THE BALCONY. If you please—don't call poets gentlemen. Poets are not gentlemen.

DR. HINKFUSS. (*Straight off.*) Nor for that matter are critics. In this sense at least. But still I call them gentlemen—out of a certain polemical affectation that, without really offending anyone, in this case at least I can be allowed. A hunger, I was saying, that these gentlemen, the poets, profoundly err in not trying to satisfy. It is

indeed deplorable that the invention of our poets, far behind everyone else, no longer succeeds in discovering ad-
equate nourishment for this vast machine we call the
theatre that, like other machines, has in recent years
enormously and wondrously grown and developed. I
would not have you think that I consider the theatre mere
spectacle. *Art* it is indeed—but *life* as well. Creation it is
indeed—but not enduring creation. A thing of the moment. A miracle. A statue that moves. A miracle, ladies
and gentlemen, that can by its very nature only be of the
moment, transitory, caught up in time. To create, in a
single moment, before your eyes, a scene—and within this
one, another, and within this, still another, and within this,
still another yet. A moment of darkness—a sudden change
—a suggestive play of light. Here, I'll do it right before
you. (*He claps his hands and commands.*) Lights out!
(*The stage is dark. The* CURTAINS *are slightly drawn behind* DR. HINKFUSS'S *shoulders. The LIGHTS in the
theatre go up while the BUZZERS in the lobby ring to
recall the audience to their seats. In the event that everyone in the audience left the theatre, and* DR. HINKFUSS,
*simultaneous performances both in the lobby and onstage
not taking place, was compelled to wait for the return of
the audience into the theatre to commence the staging of
the airfield scene and its consequent chatter, it is of course
understood that the* CURTAINS *are not at this point drawn
and that he, before the whole audience already seated in
the theatre, will order the light out and give the other
directions necessary for going on with the performance.
Here, one assumes that both performances, in the lobby
and onstage, have, as one would wish, been given at the
same time. One should indeed try and find a way to make
this possible. The* CURTAINS *are closed, and the LIGHTS
come up again in the theatre.* DR. HINKFUSS *continues.*)
Let us wait till all the audience are in their seats again.
We must also allow time for Signora Ignazio and her
daughters, accompanied by their young officer friends, to
get back home after the theatre. (*Turning to* THE GEN-
TLEMAN IN THE BALCONY, *who by now is again in his*

seat.) Meanwhile, if you, my dear sir, my intrepid and dauntless interruptor, might wish to inform those who remained here in their seats whether anything new was disclosed in the lobby—

THE GENTLEMAN IN THE BALCONY. Are you speaking to me, sir?

DR. HINKFUSS. Yes, to you. If you could be so kind as to—

THE GENTLEMAN IN THE BALCONY. No, nothing new to speak of. Simply a rather charming diversion. They all gossiped about each other. The only thing was that one learned that this clown Palmiro, Sampognetta, is crazy about that night club singer.

DR. HINKFUSS. Ah, yes. But then this one could already have deduced. Anyhow, it has little importance.

THE YOUNG SPECTATOR IN THE ORCHESTRA. No, I'm sorry, one also came to realize that that Officer Rico Verri—

THE LEADING ACTOR. (*Pushing his head between the* CURTAINS *and over the shoulder of* DR. HINKFUSS.) That's quite enough of this officer business. I'll soon be out of this uniform.

DR. HINKFUSS. (*Turning around to* THE LEADING ACTOR, *who has already pulled his head back in.*) May I please ask why you are interrupting us in this fashion?

THE LEADING ACTOR. (*Sticking his head out again.*) Because this tag gripes me and I want to get things straight right now. I am not an officer. Not by profession, that is. I am a reserve officer. (*He draws his head back in again.*)

DR. HINKFUSS. You made this quite clear some time ago. That's quite enough. (*Turning again to* THE YOUNG SPECTATOR IN THE ORCHESTRA.) I'm very sorry. Excuse me. You were saying—?

THE YOUNG SPECTATOR IN THE ORCHESTRA. (*Intimidated and embarrassed.*) Nothing really— I was just saying that—that even out there, in the lobby, this Signor Verri made it quite clear that he has a very bad temper and that—and that he's beginning to get fed up with the scandals these young ladies and their mother are always creating—

DR. HINKFUSS. Yes, yes, that's very good. But this, too, one could have guessed right from the start. In any case, thank you very much, very much indeed. (*Behind the* CURTAIN *is heard the sound of a piano playing Siebel's aria from Faust: "Le parlate d'amor—o cari fior—"*) There—that's the piano. Everything's ready now. (*He pushes back the* CURTAIN *a little and yells behind stage.*) Buzzer. Buzzer. (*At the sound of the BUZZER he goes back down into his seat in the orchestra, and the* CURTAIN *opens again.*)

ACT THREE

At the Right, in the rear, is the frame of a wall made of panes of glass, with a door in the middle through which one catches a glimpse—a bit of color, a lit lamp—of the hall beyond. The set is divided in half by another wall; this too with an open door in the middle that leads from the living room at the Right into the dining room. The dining room is roughly sketched in, with a pretentious sideboard, a table spread with a red cloth over which hangs, from the ceiling a lamp, now extinguished, with an enormous bellshaped shade of orange and green. On the sideboard, among other things, are a candlestick with a candle in it, a box of matches, and a cork bottlestopper. In the living room, besides the piano, are a sofa, a few small tables, and some chairs.

When the CURTAINS part, POMARICI is seen seated at the piano playing. NENE is waltzing to the music with SARELLI, and DORINA with NARDI. They have just returned from the theatre. Because of a toothache, SIGNORA IGNAZIA has a black silk handkerchief tied around her face like a bandage. RICO VERRI has run to an all-night pharmacy looking for medicine that might made the toothache go away. MOMMINA is seated beside her mother on the sofa. Near them is POMETTI. TOTINA is offstage with MANGINI.

MOMMINA. (*To her mother, while* POMARICI *continues to play and the couples to dance.*) Does it hurt terribly? (*She starts to put her hand to her mother's cheek.*)

SIGNORA IGNAZIA. I am going mad! Don't touch me!

POMETTI. Verri's gone to the drugstore. He'll be back any minute with something.

SIGNORA IGNAZIA. Oh. they won't open up for him! They won't open up for him!

MOMMINA. But they have to. It's an all-night drug store, isn't it?

SIGNORA IGNAZIA. Indeed! Indeed! As though you didn't know perfectly well what people are like in this town! Ayi! Ayi! Don't make me talk. I am going mad! They're quite capable of not opening up at all, if they find out it's for me.

POMETTI. Oh, you just wait and see. Verri will make them open up. He's quite capable of knocking the door down if they don't.

NENE. (*Calmly, continuing to dance.*) Of course, Mama. You can be sure of that.

DORINA. (*In the same tone.*) Think of them not opening up! If he puts himself to it he is more beastly than they are!

SIGNORA IGNAZIA. No, no, poor boy. Don't talk like that. He's so good. He went right away.

MOMMINA. He did. Only he did it. All by himself. The rest of you kept right on dancing.

SIGNORA IGNAZIA. Let them, let them dance. At any rate the pain will not go away if they stand around asking me how I am (*To* POMETTI.) It's the rage, it's the rage that these people in town arise in me; just fire in my blood. They are the cause of all my grief.

NENE. (*Stops dancing and turns to her mother, excited by the idea she has to propose.*) Mama, and if you said the Ave Maria like the other time?

POMETTI. There you have it! That's an idea!

NENE. (*Persisting.*) Don't you remember how the pain went away as soon as you said it?

POMETTI. Come on, give it a try, Signora. Give it a try.

DORINA. (*As she continues to dance.*) Yes, yes, do, Mama. You'll see, the pain'll go away.

NENE. Yes, but you must stop dancing.

POMETTI. Sure, and Pomarici stop playing.

NENE. Mama's going to say the Ave Maria like the other time!

POMARICI. (*Getting up from the piano and rushing*

over.) Fine. Fine. Let's see if we can get that miracle repeated.

SARELLI. And do it in Latin. In Latin, Signora Ignazia.

NARDI. Sure. It'll have more effect in Latin.

SIGNORA IGNAZIA. No, no, let me alone. What is it you're asking me to do?

NENE. But, Mama, you know it worked the other time. It went away then.

DORINA. We have to do it in the dark, too! In the dark.

NENE. And we must all get in a group! Pomarici, turn off the lights.

POMARICI. But where's Totina?

DORINA. She's in the other room with Mangini. Stop thinking about Totina and turn off the lights.

SIGNORA IGNAZIA. Not at all. We have to have a candle at least. And hands where they should be. And Totina must come back in here.

MOMMINA. (*Calling.*) Totina! Totina!

DORINA. There's a candle out there.

NENE. You go get it. I'm going for the little statue of the Madonna.

(*She runs off to the rear.* DORINA *goes into the dining room with* NARDI *to get the candle off the sideboard. Before lighting it, in the dark,* NARDI *embraces* DORINA *and kisses her passionately.*)

SIGNORA IGNAZIA. (*Yelling back to* NENE *who is already offstage.*) No, no, don't bother. Forget it. Why the Madonna? We don't need all that.

POMARICI. (*Also yelling back at* NENE.) Make Totina come back in, instead.

SIGNORA IGNAZIA. Yes, that's right. Totina, here! Right away!

POMETTI. We need a little table for the altar. (*He goes and gets it.*)

DORINA. (*Coming back with the candle lit, as* POMARICI *turns off the LIGHT.*) Here's the candle.

POMETTI. Put it here on the table.

NENE. (*From the rear, with the little statue of the Madonna.*) And here's the Madonna.

POMARICI. And Totina?

NENE. She's coming now. Don't be silly calling Totina all the time

SIGNORA IGNAZIA. Could we know just what they're doing in there?

NENE. Nothing, really. Getting ready with a surprise. You'll see. (*Then bidding* EVERYONE *with her gesture.*) Here, back in here. Everyone, get close to her. Concentrate, Mama.

(*Tableau: In the darkness, scarcely lessened by the quavering light of the candle,* DR. HINKFUSS *has prepared a most exquisite effect: the suffusion of a gentle green "miracle light"—psychological effect, of course—almost as though it was emanating from the hope that the miracle take place. All this almost at the very moment* SIGNORA IGNAZIA, *seated before the Madonna that has been placed with the candle on the little table, begins, with clasped hands, to recite, in a slow, deep voice, the words of the prayer, half expecting, after each word, that the pain will pass.*)

SIGNORA IGNAZIA. Ave Maria, Gratia plena, Dominus tecum—

(*Suddenly thunder and the devilish glare of a bright red light breaks up everything.* TOTINA, *dressed as a man, in* MANGINI'S *uniform, enters singing, followed by* MANGINI *who has put on a very long bathrobe, belonging to Signor Palmiro. One realizes almost at once that the thunder is the voice of* TOTINA *singing and the red light is the light that* MANGINI *turns on in the living room coming in.*)

TOTINA. "Le parlate d'amor—O cari fior—"

(*A loud and unanimous cry of protest.*)

NENE. You fool. Shut up.

MOMMINA. She has spoiled everything!

TOTINA. (*Stunned.*) What's the matter?

DORINA. Mama was saying the Ave Maria.

TOTINA. (*To* NENE.) You *could* have told me!

NENE. Is that so? Was I to guess you'd come crashing in at just this very moment?

TOTINA. I was already dressed up when you came and got the Madonna.

NENE. Well then, you should have guessed what we were doing.

DORINA. Enough, enough! What do we do now?

POMARICI. Start all over again; start all over again.

SIGNORA IGNAZIA. I don't know. I'm not sure—

MOMMINA. (*Happily.*) Has it gone?

SIGNORA IGNAZIA. I don't know. Maybe it was the devil —or the Madonna— (*Her whole face is contorted in a new fit of pain.*) No. No. Ayi! Ayi! Again. I thought it was gone. Ayyyyyiiiii! Good God, what torture! (*All of a sudden getting hold of herself, grinding her heel into the floor and commanding.*) No! I'll not give in! Sing. sing, girls! Sing, boys! Do me this favor. Sing! Woe if I'll lose my nerve because of an infernal toothache! Go ahead, Mommina. "Stride la vampa!"

MOMMINA. (*While* EVERYONE, *applauding, yells,* "Yes, yes, that's it, the chorus from 'Trovatore.'") No, no, Mama. I don't feel like it. No.

SIGNORA IGNAZIA. (*Angrily insisting.*) Do me this one favor, Mommina. It's for the tooth's ache.

NENE. Come on. Please her just this once.

TOTINA. She's telling you she's trying to keep her courage up under the pain.

SARELLI *and* NARDI. Yes, yes. Come on. Humor her, Mommina

DORINA. God, how you like to be coaxed!

NENE. You think we don't know why you don't want to sing any more?

POMARICI. No, no. Mommina *will* sing.

SARELLI. If it's on account of Verri, don't you worry. We'll see to it that he keeps in his place.

POMARICI. Singing will charm away the pain! I swear it!

SIGNORA IGNAZIA. Yes, yes. Do it. Do it for your poor mama's sake.

POMETTI. What terrific courage the general's got.

SIGNORA IGNAZIA. You, Totina, will be Manrico?

TOTINA. Of course. I'm already dressed for it!

SIGNORA IGNAZIA. Paint the moustache on her. Paint the moustache on this girl.

MANGINI Here, I'll do it myself.

POMARICI. No, if you please, *I'll* do it.

NENE. Here's the cork, Pomarici. I'll go get the big hat with the feather. And a yellow handkerchief and a red shawl for Azucena. (*She leaves by the rear and returns a moment later with the objects she spoke of.*)

POMARICI. (*To* TOTINA, *as he paints on the moustache.*) Stay still, please.

SIGNORA IGNAZIA. Wonderful, Mommina as Azucena—

MOMMINA. (*By this time speaking almost to herself but without strength left to refuse.*) No, no, no—I can't—

SIGNORA IGNAZIA. (*Continuing.*) Totina as Manrico—

SARELLI. And the rest of us the gypsy chorus!

SIGNORA IGNAZIA. (*Commencing the music.*) "All'opra, all'opra! Dagli. Martella. Chi del gitana la vita abbella?" (*Singing, she asks some of them the question. They keep looking at her, uncertain whether she is asking them seriously or jokingly. And then turning to others she repeats.*) "Chi del gitano la vita abbella?" (*But these too look at her as the others did. She can endure her pain no longer and furiously she once again asks all of them, insisting on a reply.*) "Chi del gitano la vita abbella?"

ALL. (*Understanding at last, intone the reply.*) "La zingareeee--eeeella!'"

SIGNORA IGNAZIA. (*Taking a deep breath at finally being understood.*) Ahhhhhhhhhhhh! (*Then while* THE OTHERS *hold the note, to herself, writhing in pain.*) Let me get hold of myself! I can't stand it any more. Go ahead, go ahead! Children, quick, sing, sing!

POMARICI. No, wait, for God's sake, till I finish.

DORINA. More than this? That's enough!

SARELLI. She looks marvelous.

NENE. Adorable! Now for the hat! The hat! (*She gives it to her and turns to* MOMMINA.) And you, no more excuses! Put the handkerchief on your head! (*To* SARELLI.) Tie it in back for her. (SARELLI *does so.*) And the shawl. Like this.

DORINA. (*Giving* MOMMINA, *who has remained immobile, a shake.*) Wake up. Come to!

POMARICI Oh, but we have to have something to beat time on!

NENE. I know just the thing. Those brass finger-bowls in there. (*She goes and gets them from the sideboard in the dining room. She returns and hands them out.*)

POMARICI. (*Going to the piano.*) Now attention. We're starting from the beginning. "Vedi le fosche notturne spoglie." (*He begins to play the gypsy chorus that opens the second act of "Il Trovatore."*)

CHORUS. (*On the beat.*)

> "Vedi le fosche notturne spoglie
> de' cieli sveste l'immensa volta:
> sembra una vedova che alfin si toglie
> i bruni panni ond' era involta."
>   (*Then beating the fingerbowls.*)
> "All'opra, all'opra! Dagli. Martella.
> Chi del gitano la vita abbella?"
>   (*And three times.*)
> "La zingarella!"

POMARICI. (*To* MOMMINA.) Attention, Miss. Mommina, it's your turn. And all of you get around her.

MOMMINA. (*Coming forward.*)

> "Stride la vampa! la folla indomita
> corre a quel foco. lieta in sembianza!
> Urli di gioja intorno echeggiano:
> cinta di sgherri donna s'avanza."

(*While* The Others *are singing, first* The Chorus *and then* Mommina *alone,* Signora Ignazio, *seated in a chair, squirming constantly, beating her feet, first one and then the other, mutters in cadenza, as if in her pain she was reciting a litany.*)

Signora Ignazio. God, I'm dying, dying. Have pity on my sins. God, God, what agony! Hit me, God! Make me suffer, yes, me alone! Make me alone pay, God, for all the amusements the girls have. Sing, sing, yes, yes, enjoy yourselves, girls! I'll sit here and suffer all alone. It's penance for my sins. I want you happy, gay, gay, just like this. Yes, "dagli, martella," hit me, me alone, dear God, and let the girls enjoy themselves. Oh, God, the joy I never had—never, never, God, never, never—I want *them* to have it. They *should. Should* have it. *I'll* pay for it. Yes, I'll pay for everything, God, even if they break your commandments, dear God. (*She joins in with* The Others *while the tears trickle down her cheeks.*) "La zingareeee—eeeéllaaaaa!" Silence. Now Mommina's singing, the voice of a true *artiste.* "La vampa"—yes. Ah, that's what I've got in my jaw, fire, fire! "Lieta, yes, lieta in sembianza"—

(Rico Verri *unexpectedly appears in the door at the rear. For a moment he stands there suspended, as if his bewilderment were a precipice opened up before his anger. Then he leaps into the room and rushes up to* Pomarici. *He yanks him off the piano stool and hurls him to the floor, yelling.*)

Rico Verri. God damn you all! So this is the way you make fun of me behind my back, is it?

(*There follows at first a bewilderment in them all that is expressed by certain silly and incongruous exclamations.*)

Nene. But just look at his manners!

DORINA. Are you crazy?

(*Then a general uproar, as* POMARICI *gets up and throws himself on* VERRI *and* THE OTHERS *get between them, trying to separate them and keep them apart.* EVERYONE *talks at once, in great confusion.*)

POMARICI. You'll pay for this, Verri!

VERRI. (*Violently pushing him back.*) I'm not through with you yet!

SARELLI *and* NARDI. We're here, too. You'll answer us for this, too.

VERRI. Every damned one of you. I'll break all your noses.

TOTINA. Who made you master in our house?

VERRI. I was sent out to get medicine for her tooth—

SIGNORA IGNAZIA. The medicine, yes, and—?

VERRI. (*Pointing to* MOMMINA.) And I come back and find her dressed up like this.

SIGNORA IGNAZIA. Get out of my house this minute!

MOMMINA. I didn't want to. I didn't want to. I told everyone I didn't want to.

DORINA. Look what we have here. The little fool's apologizing to him.

NENE. He's just taking advantage of the fact we have no man in our house to kick him out. That's what he deserves.

SIGNORA IGNAZIA. (*To* NENE.) Go get your father immediately. Make him get up and come in here at once.

SARELLI. If that's what you want, Signora, we can throw him out.

NENE. (*Running to call her father.*) Papa, Papa. (*She runs off.*)

VERRI. (*To* SARELLI.) You? I'd like to see you. Go ahead and throw me out! (*To* NENE *as she runs off.*) Yes, call Papa, call him. I'll answer the head of this house for what I'm doing—demanding from *them* a little respect for you ladies.

SIGNORA IGNAZIA. And who has asked you to? How dare you demand it?

VERRI. How? The Signorina knows. (*He points to* MOMMINA.)

MOMMINA. Oh, but not like this, with such violence.

VERRI. Am I the one who's being violent? Isn't it the *others* towards *you?*

SIGNORA IGNAZIA. I repeat. I want to know nothing about all this! There's the door. Get out!

VERRI. You can't say this to me.

SIGNORA IGNAZIA. My daughter will also tell you this. Anyhow, I am the lady of the house and *I* command.

DORINA We'll all say the same thing to you.

VERRI That's not enough. Not if the Signorina's with me. I'm the only man in this room with—honorable intentions!

SARELLI. Listen to him! *Honorable!*

NARDI. No one's doing a thing here he shouldn't!

VERRI. The Signorina knows the truth.

POMARICI. Buffoon!

VERRI. Buffoons. the god-damned lot of you! (*Brandishing a chair*) Watch out—don't any of you butt in or it'll end right now.

POMETTI. (*To the* OTHERS.) Come on. Let's get out of here.

DORINA. No Why?

TOTINA. Don't leave us alone. He's not the master in our house.

VERRI. You, Nardi, don't you feign any sickness tomorrow. We've got a date.

NENE. (*Returning in great distress.*) Papa's not in the house!

SIGNORA IGNAZIA. Not in the house?

NENE. I've looked all over. I can't find him anywhere.

DORINA. What's this? Didn't he come home?

NENE. He didn't come home.

MOMMINA. Where is he?

SIGNORA IGNAZIA. Still out, at this hour?

SARELLI. He must have gone back to the night club.

POMARICI. Signora, we're leaving.

SIGNORA IGNAZIA. No, wait—

MANGINI. Of course, wait. I certainly can't leave like this!

TOTINA. Oh, I'm sorry. I'd completely forgotten I had your uniform on. I'll go and change right away. (*She slips away.*)

POMARICI. (*To* MANGINI.) You wait and get your uniform. We're going on.

SIGNORA IGNAZIA. But excuse me—I don't understand—

VERRI. They understand. They understand all right, even if you, Signora, don't choose to.

SIGNORA IGNAZIA. I'll tell you once more. You're the one who's getting out of here.

VERRI. No, Signora, they must leave. They know there's no place here any more for their dirty jokes—face to face with a man who has serious intentions.

POMARICI. Yeah, yeah, you'll see tomorrow whether we're joking or not!

MOMMINA. Please, Verri. Please!

VERRI. (*Trembling.*) You should not plead, *anyone!*

MOMMINA. I'm not pleading. I only want to say that the fault's all mine, who gave in. I shouldn't have, knowing that you—

NARDI. As an earnest, upright Sicilian, couldn't take a joke.

SARELLI. We aren't taking any more jokes now, either.

VERRI. (*To* MOMMINA, *as he would speak to* THE LEADING ACTRESS, *by now spontaneously coming out of his part, with the irritation of* THE LEADING ACTOR *who has been forced to say what he does not wish to say.*) *Excellent. Are you pleased?*

MOMMINA. (*As* THE LEADING ACTRESS, *disconcerted.*) With what?

VERRI. (*As before.*) With having said what you shouldn't have. Why does all this guilt come in right here at the end?

MOMMINA. It just came to me spontaneously.

VERRI. And doing so you made them start in on me again! It's I who must be the last one to shout that they have to deal with me, every one of them.

MANGINI. Even I, like this, in a bathrobe? (*He arches his legs clumsily as though on guard.*) Pronto. Opla!

NENE *and* DORINA. (*Laughing and applauding.*) Oh, that's lovely! Bravo!

VERRI. (*As before, indignantly.*) What do you mean, "bravo"? Idiocy! That's how the whole scene gets spoiled. And it will never come to an end!

DR. HINKFUSS. (*Getting up from his seat in the orchestra.*) Why not? It was all going very, very well. Keep on. Keep on.

(*There is heard, getting increasingly louder, a knock in the hall at the back, as though on the street door.*)

MANGINI. (*Excusing himself.*) I am standing here in a bathrobe. What's more natural than to make a joke?

NENE. But of course.

VERRI. (*Scornfully to* MANGINI.) Go play cards or something, then. Don't come here to act!

MOMMINA. If Mr. —————— (*She says the name of* THE LEADING ACTOR.) would like to play his role all by himself, while we sit here and twiddle our thumbs, let him say so, and we can all leave.

VERRI. No, it's I who must leave, if everyone else wants to do things *his* way, the way that suits *him;* even to timing everything all wrong!

SIGNORA IGNAZIA. But good heavens, it was beautiful, our timing was perfect. You know it was. That cry of Mommina's: "The fault's mine, who gave in—"

POMARICI. (*To* VERRI.) Look here, after all, we're in this show too, you know.

SARELLI. We must live *our* parts, too.

NARDI. He wants to be the whole show all by himself. But everyone's got to say what he has to say.

DR. HINKFUSS. (*Yelling.*) Enough. This is quite enough. Get on with the scene. It seems to me that it is

exactly you, Mr. ———— (*The name of* THE LEADING
ACTOR.), who has spoiled everything.

VERRI. No, no, please, I do indeed want everyone to
speak who ought to, and to answer me just as he should.
For three hours I keep hammering at the same thing:
"The Signorina knows, the Signorina knows—" And the
Signorina does not find one single word to back me up.
Always this same old pose of martyred victim.

MOMMINA. (*Exasperated, almost in tears.*) But I am,
I *am* the victim! The victim of my sisters, of the house,
of you; the victim of everyone.

(*At this point, pushing between* THE ACTORS *all turned
towards the footlights to speak with* DR. HINKFUSS,
THE CHARACTER ACTOR, *or rather* SAMPOGNETTA,
*makes his way; his face like a dead man's; his
bloody hands on his stomach, where he has been
wounded by a knife; his coat and trousers smeared
with blood.*)

SAMPOGNETTA. Look here, Dr. Hinkfuss. I'm standing
out there knocking, knocking, knocking. Smeared with
blood, like this. I've got my guts in my fists, and I'm supposed to come in here and die. Onstage. Which isn't very
easy anyhow for a character actor. And no one lets me
in. When I finally do get in, what do I find? Complete
and utter confusion. The whole effect I've been promising
myself I'd create with my entrance is completely ruined.
I'm dripping with blood, and dying, and I'm drunk, too.
I ask you, *now* what do I do?

DR. HINKFUSS. It's all very simple. You're leaning on
the shoulder of the night club singer. Where is she?

NIGHT CLUB SINGER. Here I am.

ONE OF THE CUSTOMERS FROM THE NIGHT CLUB. I'm
here, too, to help hold him up.

DR. HINKFUSS. Very well. Hold him up.

SAMPOGNETTA. I had the stairs to climb, carried on the
shoulders of these two—

DR. HINKFUSS. Good God. Pretend all that's been

done. And each of you get back in your places. And all
of you begin to cry in despair. Can you drown in a tea
cup? (*He returns to his seat muttering to himself.*) And
all this ruined for a silly punctilious point of view.

(*The action is resumed.* SAMPOGNETTA *appears now at
the rear, supported by the* NIGHT CLUB SINGER *on
one side and the* THE CUSTOMER FROM THE NIGHT
CLUB *on the other. Almost the first moment* SIGNORA
IGNAZIA *and the* DAUGHTERS *see him, they suddenly
start screaming. But* SAMPOGNETTA *remains motionless while the women vent their feelings, a tolerant
smile playing on his lips that seems to say, "When
you're done, I shall speak." He lets the* NIGHT CLUB
SINGER *and* THE CUSTOMER FROM THE NIGHT CLUB
*make a few replies to the anguished questions with
which he is overwhelmed, even though he would
clearly prefer for them to be quiet and wait for the
truth he himself is visibly preparing to disclose when
everyone else has finished speaking. The* OTHERS,
*seeing him before them in such a subdued manner,
do not have the least idea what he intends to do and
play their parts as best they can.*)

SIGNORA IGNAZIA. Oh God, what's happened?
MOMMINA. Papa, my Papa!
NENE. You've been wounded!
VERRI. Who did it?
DORINA. Where is he wounded? Where?
THE CUSTOMER. In the belly.
SARELLI. With a knife?
NIGHT CLUB SINGER. Ripped right open. He's lost all
his blood getting here.
NARDI. But who did it? Who did it?
POMETTI. Was it at the night club?
MANGINI. Get him to lie down, for Christ's sake.
POMARICI. Here. Over here on the sofa.
SIGNORA IGNAZIA. ·(*As the* NIGHT CLUB SINGER *and*

THE CUSTOMER *take* SAMPOGNETTA *over to the sofa*.) So he did go back to the night club. Didn't he?

NENE. But, Mama, don't talk about it now. Can't you see he's wounded?

SIGNORA IGNAZIA. I see how he's come home, all right —and look, look, at the clutch she's got on him. Who are you?

NIGHT CLUB SINGER. A woman, Signora, with more of a heart than you.

THE CUSTOMER. Think, Signora, it's your own husband who stands here dying.

MOMMINA. But how did it happen? How did it happen?

THE CUSTOMER. He was trying to defend her— (*He indicates the* NIGHT CLUB SINGER.)

SIGNORA IGNAZIA. (*With a sardonic smile.*) There, see! He thinks he's Sir Galahad!

THE CUSTOMER. (*Continuing.*) A fight started—

NIGHT CLUB SINGER. And that cutthroat—

THE CUSTOMER. Turned from her and threw himself on *him!*

VERRI. Did they get him?

THE CUSTOMER. No, he got away, waving his knife wildly at everyone.

NARDI. At least you know who he is?

THE CUSTOMER. (*Gesturing to the* NIGHT CLUB SINGER.) She knows him very well—

SARELLI. Your lover?

NIGHT CLUB SINGER. My murderer! My murderer!

THE CUSTOMER. He was ready for a massacre.

NENE. But someone has to go and get a doctor right away!

(TOTINA *appears, still only half dressed.*)

TOTINA. What's happened? What's happened? Oh God, Papa! Who wounded him?

MOMMINA. Speak, speak, Papa, say *something*—

DORINA. Why are you staring at us like that?

NENE. He just stares at us and smiles.

TOTINA. But where did it happen? How did it happen?

SIGNORA IGNAZIA. (*To* TOTINA.) At the night club. Now don't you understand? (*She points to the* NIGHT CLUB SINGER.) Of course!

NENE. A doctor, a doctor! We can't let him die like this.

MOMMINA. Who'll go and get one?

MANGINI. I'd go, except that like this— (*He motions to the bathrobe.*)

TOTINA. Oh, I'd forgotten. Go get your uniform. It's in there on the bed.

NENE. You go, Sarelli, please.

SARELLI. Yes, yes, of course. I'm off. I'm off. (*He goes off rear with* MANGINI.)

VERRI. But why doesn't he say a word? (*He is alluding to* SAMPOGNETTA.) He ought to say *something—*

TOTINA. Papa! Papa!

NENE. He keeps on looking at us and smiling.

MOMMINA. Papa, here we all are, at your side!

VERRI. Could it be that's what he wants—to die without saying a word?

POMARICI. This is fine. He stands there neither dead nor alive. What in God's name is he waiting for?

NARDI. I can't think of another thing to do. Sarelli's gone to get the doctor and Mangini to get his uniform.

SIGNORA IGNAZIA. (*To her* HUSBAND.) Speak up! Speak up! Don't you even have brains enough to say a solitary word? If you'd only listened to me, if you'd only stopped to think you had four little girls at home who now very well may go without a bite of bread to eat—

NENE. (*Having waited a moment, with the* OTHERS.) Not a word, nothing. Look at him there! He just smiles.

MOMMINA. It isn't natural. (*Meaning his acting.*)

DORINA. You can't just smile like that, Papa, and stare at us.

THE CUSTOMER. Maybe he drunk a little too much—

MOMMINA. It isn't natural. If someone has a drink and it makes him sad, then he's quiet and peaceful. But if it makes him smile, then he talks. He shouldn't be smiling, then!

SIGNORA IGNAZIA. Can you at least tell us why you are smiling like this?

(*Once more they* ALL *wait in suspense.*)

SAMPOGNETTA. Because I'm simply delighted by the fact that all of you are much, much better actors than I.

VERRI. (*As the* OTHERS *look at each other, all suddenly frozen in their make-believe.*) But what is he saying?

SAMPOGNETTA. I'm saying that I, like this, having no idea how I got in this house if no one came to let me in, and after I'd stood there at the door knocking so long and so hard—

DR. HINKFUSS. (*Furiously getting up from his seat.*) Again? The same thing all over again?

SAMPOGNETTA. I simply cannot die like this, Dr. Hinkfuss. I can't help smiling, seeing how good they all are, and I just don't die. The maid—(*He looks around.*) where is *she?* I don't see her—should have run in and cried, "Oh God, the Master. Oh God, the Master! They're bringing him home wounded!"

DR. HINKFUSS. But why are you harping on this now? Didn't we say we'd take your entrance for granted?

SAMPOGNETTA. Now all I have to do then is die, die without a word.

DR. HINKFUSS. Not at all. You must speak. You must have a big scene—and *then* die.

SAMPOGNETTA. All right. We've had the scene. We'll take that for granted, too. (*He drops back on the sofa.*) I'm dead!

DR. HINKFUSS. Not like that!

SAMPOGNETTA. (*Getting up on his feet and coming toward the footlights.*) My dear sir, then *you* come up here and finish me off. What do you want me to say? I repeat, I can't die just like that, without help from anyone. I am not, please remember, some old accordion that you push

and pull, that comes up with a tune everytime you press
on the keys.

DR. HINKFUSS. But your colleagues—

SAMPOGNETTA. (*Quickly*.) Are more gifted than I. I
admit the fact quite freely, and it delights me. I cannot
do it. The scene-entrance was everything for me. You
dropped it. And without the maid's cry, I cannot get into
the right feeling. And then—Death himself should have
entered into the room with me, introducing himself here
into the shameless uproar of my own house; Death the
drunkard, as we'd already established it, drunk with a
wine that turns to blood. And I should have spoken, yes,
that I know—tried to speak in the midst of all this hor-
ror—taking courage from the wine, and the blood, supported only by this woman here (*Going over to the*
NIGHT CLUB SINGER *and leaning on her, his arm around
her neck*.) like this!—saying wild, senseless, terrible
things to my wife, and to my daughters, and to these
young men. I should have proved to them all that if I've
behaved like a fool, it's because they've been vile—vile
wife, vile daughters, vile friends. I'm not a fool. It is I
who am good. It is they who are bad; only I who am
intelligent, and they who are stupid; I, in all my clever-
ness, and they, in their corrupt bestiality, yes, yes—
(*Growing angry as though someone were contradicting
him*.) intelligent, intelligent, as babes are intelligent—
(well, not all of them—those who grew up, heartbroken
in the midst of the adult brutality). But I should have
said all these things like a drunkard, in a delirium, and
smeared my bloody hands on my face—like this—and be-
fouled myself with blood—(*Asking the* OTHER AC-
TORS.) am I smeared with blood? (*And as they nod yes*.)
Good—(*And resuming*.) terrify you all and make you
cry—but *really* cry—hardly able to get my breath and
puckering up my lips like this (*He tries to form a whistle
that does not come: ſhhhhh, ſhhhhh*.) to make my very
last little whistle and then—(*Calling* THE CUSTOMER
over to him.) you come here, too—(*He hangs onto his
neck with his other arm*.) like this—between the two of

you—but nearer you, sweetheart—drop my head, the quick little way birds do, and die. (*He drops his head on the breast of the* NIGHT CLUB SINGER. *His arms go limp after a moment, and he falls on the floor dead.*)

NIGHT CLUB SINGER. Oh God! (*She tries to hold him up and then lets go of him.*) He's dead! He's dead!

MOMMINA. (*Throwing herself on him.*) Papa, my Papa, my Papa— (*And she begins to cry. This outburst of actual emotion in* THE LEADING ACTRESS *provokes emotion in the* OTHER ACTORS, *who give themselves up to tears, too. And then* DR. HINKFUSS *leaps up from his seat shouting.*)

DR. HINKFUSS. Excellent. Lights out, please. Lights out. (*The stage is darkened.*) Everyone offstage. The four sisters and their mother around the dining table, six days later. The living room is dark. The only light is from the lamp in the dining room.

MOMMINA. (*In the dark.*) But, Dr. Hinkfuss, we have to change costumes first. We're supposed to be in mourning.

DR. HINKFUSS. Ah, yes. In mourning. The curtains should have been dropped after the death scene. It does not matter. Go and get in your mourning clothes. And drop the curtains. Lights up in the theatre, please. (*The* CURTAINS *are closed. The LIGHTS in the theatre come up.* DR. HINKFUSS *smiles sadly.*) We've lost part of the effect to be sure. But I promise you we'll get it all tomorrow evening. And it will be truly overwhelming. You must know, ladies and gentlemen, that in life as well, an effect one has worked at and counted on can, even at best, just not come off—and then our reproaches go to the wife, to the daughters. "You ought to have done this!" and "You ought to have done that!" It's true that here it was a question of death. It's a shame my fine Mr. ———— (*He names* THE CHARACTER ACTOR.) was so stubborn about his entrance. But he's a good actor. Tomorrow evening he'll acquit himself of the scene marvelously. And a great scene it is, ladies and gentlemen, for all the consequences it brings. I made it up myself. It isn't in the story at all and, moreover, I'm sure the author would never have put it in, for scruples I myself had no reason to respect: those of spreading the idea, already quite widespread, that in Sicily the knife is very much used. If he'd had the idea at all that the character should die, he would have had him die of a stroke, or a heart attack, or some such thing as that. But you yourselves can see what a different sort of theatrical effect you get from the death as *I* have conceived it, with the wine, and the blood, and his arm around the neck of that singer. The father has to die. Through his death the family falls into wretched poverty. Without that it seems highly unlikely that Mommina would ever consent to marry that Rico Verri, resisting every objection her mother and sisters can possibly raise. They have learned, from a few questions sent to the town he comes from, that he is, yes, from a very well-to-do family, but that his father is infamous in the whole area not only as an outrageous miser but also as a man so possessed by jealousy that he had, in a few short years, made his poor wife—Rico Verri's mother—die of a broken heart. And can you imagine the fate awaiting this sweet young girl? Think of all the things Rico Verri, marrying the girl out of spite to get even with his fellow officers, must have agreed on with that jealous, stingy, old father of his? And the other promises he must have made to himself, not only to recompense himself for the sacrifice his honor was costing him but also to be able to face his fellow townsmen, to whom the notoriety of his wife's family was all too well known. Who knows how he will make her pay for the pleasure she's gotten out of life the years she was living at home with her mother and her sisters? His feelings are quite reasonable, as you shall see. But my gifted heroine, Miss ———— (*He names* THE LEADING ACTRESS.) is not really of my opinion. Mommina is for her the most aware of the four sisters, the one who has been sacrificed, who has always arranged amusements for the others but who herself has never enjoyed any except at the price of effort, vigilance, and many unhappy thoughts.

The responsibility for the whole family falls on her shoulders. And she comes to an understanding of many things: first of all, that time passes, and that the father, with all the disorder at home, was unable to set aside anything for all of them, and that no young man in town will marry any of them, while Verri—ah, Verri will fight for her, not one, but three duels with those officers, who of course immediately, at the first whiff of misfortune, slip away, disappear, evaporate. At the bottom of it, the passion that makes up all melodrama—which Mommina has in common with her sisters—Raul, Ernani, Don Alvaro—"Ne toglier mi potro, l'imagin suo dal cuor—," keeps a firm attitude and marries him. (DR. HINKFUSS *has continued talking in order to give his* ACTRESSES *time to change, but now he has nothing more to say. He takes a little leap and, pulling back one of the curtains, yells inside.*) Is it really possible that the ladies still are not ready? Where's the buzzer? (*And pretending to speak with someone behind the* CURTAIN *he adds.*) No? What else must be done? What? They no longer wish to act? And what could that mean? With the audience out here waiting? Come here at once.

(DR. HINKFUSS' SECRETARY *appears, embarrassed and confused.*)

THE SECRETARY. But they say—
DR. HINKFUSS. What *is* it they say?
THE LEADING ACTOR. (*Behind the* CURTAIN, *to* THE SECRETARY.) Speak up. Speak up clearly and tell him why.
DR. HINKFUSS. Ah, Mr. ————— once again.

(*He names* THE LEADING ACTOR. *But now the* OTHER ACTORS *and* ACTRESSES *come out in front of the* CURTAIN, *beginning with* THE CHARACTER ACTRESS, *who takes off her wig in front of the audience, and* THE CHARACTER ACTOR; THE LEADING ACTOR, *next, has by this time taken off his uniform.*)

THE CHARACTER ACTRESS. No, no, Dr. Hinkfuss, it's all of us.

THE LEADING ACTRESS. We simply can't go on.

THE OTHERS. Impossible! Out of the question!

THE CHARACTER ACTOR. I've finished my part, to be sure, but I'm right here—

DR. HINKFUSS. In God's name, what's happened now?

THE CHARACTER ACTOR. (*The last phrase of* THE CHARACTER ACTOR'S *comes out tranquilly over* DR. HINKFUSS' *speech like a cold shower.*) —square behind my colleagues.

DR. HINKFUSS. Square behind your colleagues. Just what do you mean by that?

THE CHARACTER ACTOR. That we're all walking out.

DR. HINKFUSS. Walking out? Where?

SEVERAL. Out! Out!

THE LEADING ACTOR. Unless *you* do.

THE OTHERS. It's either you or us!

DR. HINKFUSS. I? *You* dare intimidate *me* like this?

THE ACTORS. All right then, we'll go! We're leaving. We're through with being puppets. Let's get out of here. (*They are wildly agitated.*)

DR. HINKFUSS. (*Parrying.*) Where? Are you mad? We've got the audience out here. They've already paid for their seats. How can you explain this to *them?*

THE CHARACTER ACTOR. You figure that one out for yourself. We're giving you a choice. You or us—

DR. HINKFUSS. I'll ask you again. *What has happened now?*

THE LEADING ACTOR. What now? Does what's already happened seem unimportant to you?

DR. HINKFUSS. But wasn't that all taken care of?

THE CHARACTER ACTOR. Taken care of how?

THE CHARACTER ACTRESS. You pretend we're improvising—

DR. HINKFUSS. It's in your contracts—

THE CHARACTER ACTOR. But look here—not like this, with you jumping up here onstage every five minutes, ordering me to die just like that—

THE CHARACTER ACTRESS. Starting us cold in the middle of a scene—

THE LEADING ACTRESS. We no longer find words—

THE LEADING ACTOR. There, just as I said at the beginning, the words ought to spring up spontaneously!

THE LEADING ACTRESS. Just a minute, my dear, you were the first one to pay no attention to the words spontaneously springing up in *me*—

THE LEADING ACTOR. You're right. But it isn't my fault.

POMARICI. Yes, he's the one who started it all.

THE LEADING ACTOR. But let me finish. I'm telling you it isn't my fault—it's *his*. (*He points to* DR. HINKFUSS.)

DR. HINKFUSS. Mine? Why mine?

THE LEADING ACTOR. Because you're here with your damned *theatre*. The devil take it.

DR. HINKFUSS. My theatre? But have you all gone crazy? Where are we? Are we not in a theatre?

THE LEADING ACTOR. We're in a theatre? Excellent. Then give us parts—

THE LEADING ACTRESS. Act by act, scene by scene—

NENE. —with speeches written, word for word—

THE CHARACTER ACTOR. Cut them as much as you like. Make us jump around just as you like. But at points designated beforehand.

THE LEADING ACTOR. First you let life loose inside us—

THE LEADING ACTRESS. Real feelings—

THE CHARACTER ACTRESS. The more we say the more excited we get—

NENE. All of us in one big uproar—

THE LEADING ACTRESS. All of us trembling—

TOTINA. (*Pointing to* THE LEADING ACTOR.) I could kill him!

DORINA. This blusterer coming in and laying down the law in our own house.

DR. HINKFUSS. But all the better, all the better that way!

THE LEADING ACTOR. What do you mean "all the better" if at the same time you insist on our being so damned careful throughout the scene—

THE CHARACTER ACTOR. —not to miss the least effect you've planned—

THE LEADING ACTOR. —because of "theatre"! How can you expect us to think any more of "theatre"—yours or anyone else's—if we must *live* our parts? Don't you see what happens? How even I got to thinking for a moment that the scene should end the way you'd told us it should, with the last line mine. And then I get in with Miss ————— (*Pointing to* THE LEADING ACTRESS *and saying her name.*) who was right, yes, absolutely right, at that point to beg—

THE LEADING ACTRESS. I was begging for you—

THE LEADING ACTOR. Yes, exactly—(*To the actor playing* MANGINI.) just as you were joking about that bathrobe—and I apologize. It's I who was stupid to have paid any attention to him. (*He points to* DR. HINKFUSS.)

DR. HINKFUSS. Watch what you say, Mr. ————— (*He names* THE LEADING ACTOR.)

THE LEADING ACTOR. (*Ignoring* DR. HINKFUSS *and again turning impetuously to* THE LEADING ACTRESS.) Don't interrupt me now—! You are truly the victim. I see it. I feel it. You are filled with your part, as I am with mine. I suffer all the agonies of hell just seeing you there before me (*He takes her face between his hands.*) with these eyes and this mouth. You're quivering all over. You're dying of fright right here in my hands. The audience is still here—we can't get rid of *them,* but we can't keep on, neither you nor I, trying to play the usual kind of theatre. As you cry out your despair, your martyrdom, I must cry out my feelings, too, the feelings that make me commit my crime. Good. Let *them* stay. They'll be like a jury hearing a case and judging it. (*With a leap he turns back to* DR. HINKFUSS.) But not you. You're getting out of here!

DR. HINKFUSS. (*Stunned.*) I?

THE LEADING ACTOR. Yes. And leave us alone. Leave the two of us alone!

NENE. Excellent.

THE CHARACTER ACTRESS. To act what they feel.

THE CHARACTER ACTOR. To act what they feel inside them. Splendid.

ALL THE OTHERS. (*Pushing* DR. HINKFUSS *off the stage.*) Yes, yes, get out, get out!

DR. HINKFUSS. You're driving me out of my own theatre?

THE CHARACTER ACTOR. We don't need you any more.

ALL THE OTHERS. (*Now pushing him down the aisle.*) Get out. Get out.

DR. HINKFUSS. This is unheard of insolence. You want to turn this into a courtroom.

THE LEADING ACTOR. Real theatre.

THE CHARACTER ACTOR. The one you scatter away every evening so all the scenes of the play could be made for the eyes alone, sensational!

THE CHARACTER ACTRESS. Theatre is real when you let your passion be alive and then a mere suggestion would be enough.

THE LEADING ACTRESS. A passionate feeling is no joking matter.

THE LEADING ACTOR. To sacrifice everything for a stage effect! You ought to do farce, not drama.

ALL THE ACTORS. Get out! Get out!

DR. HINKFUSS. I am your director.

THE LEADING ACTOR. When life comes to life it cannot be pushed around by anyone.

THE CHARACTER ACTRESS. Even the playwright has to obey it.

THE LEADING ACTRESS. Obey, yes, obey.

THE CHARACTER ACTOR. And whoever wants to give orders get out of here.

ALL THE OTHERS. Out! Out!

DR. HINKFUSS. (*With his shoulders against the exit door of the theatre.*) I'll sue! I'll sue!! I'll file charges. It's a scandal! I'm your direct—

(*He is driven out of the theatre. Meanwhile, the* CUR-

TAINS *have again opened. The stage is now dark and bare.* THE SECRETARY, THE STAGE HANDS, THE ELECTRICIANS, ALL THE BACKSTAGE PERSONNEL *have come out to see the extraordinary sight of a director driven out by his own actors.*)

THE LEADING ACTOR. (*To* THE LEADING ACTRESS, *inviting her to get back onstage.*) Come. Let's get back on. Quickly.

THE CHARACTER ACTRESS. We'll do the whole thing ourselves.

THE LEADING ACTOR. We don't need anything!

POMARICI. We'll stage the scene ourselves—

THE CHARACTER ACTOR. Good! I'll work the lights!

THE CHARACTER ACTRESS. No, it's better like this. Dark and bare.

THE LEADING ACTOR. Just enough light to outline the figures!

THE LEADING ACTRESS. And no scenery?

THE CHARACTER ACTRESS. We don't need scenery.

THE LEADING ACTRESS. Not even the walls of my jail?

THE LEADING ACTOR. Yes, but only as one can perceive them—there—for a moment—at the touch of your fingers—and then—darkness again—to illustrate after all that it is no longer the scenery that counts in the theatre.

THE CHARACTER ACTRESS. It's enough that you *feel* yourself there, child, inside your jail. It will seem to be there. Everyone will see it, just as if it really were.

THE LEADING ACTRESS. But at least I have to do something to my make-up.

THE CHARACTER ACTRESS. Wait! I have an idea! (*To* a STAGE HAND.) Go get a chair. Quickly. (STAGE HAND *exits.*)

THE LEADING ACTRESS. What are you going to do?

THE CHARACTER ACTRESS. You'll see. (*To the* OTHER ACTORS.) Meanwhile, all of you get the stage ready, but just what is barely needed. Two chairs, the small ones for the little girls, see if they are ready for us.

(THE STAGE HAND *brings in a chair.*)

THE LEADING ACTRESS. I was saying that I must change my make-up—

THE CHARACTER ACTRESS. (*Giving her the chair.*) Yes, yes. Sit here, my child.

THE LEADING ACTRESS. (*Puzzled as though she did not know where she was.*) Here?

THE CHARACTER ACTRESS. Yes, here. And you will begin to see all the sorrow— Nene, run get the make-up box and a towel. And don't forget—the nightgowns for the children.

THE LEADING ACTRESS. But what are you doing? What is all this?

THE CHARACTER ACTRESS. Leave it to us; to me, your mother, and to your sisters. We'll do your make-up ourselves. Go, Nene.

TOTINA. Get a mirror, too.

THE LEADING ACTRESS. And my dress.

DORINA. (*To* NENE, *who has already run off toward the dressing rooms.*) Get her dress, too.

THE LEADING ACTRESS. It's a skirt and coat—they're in my dressing room. (NENE *nods assent and goes off Right.*)

THE CHARACTER ACTRESS. You see, it must be our suffering—mine, your mother's who knows what age is— to make you grow old before your time—

TOTINA. And ours, who once helped make you beautiful and now shall make you ugly—

DORINA. And lay waste your loveliness—

THE LEADING ACTRESS. And condemn me for wanting that man?

THE CHARACTER ACTRESS. Yes, condemn you, but torn inside ourselves in doing so—

TOTINA. You detached yourself from us—

THE LEADING ACTRESS. But you mustn't think I did it out of fear, fear of the poverty in store for us all with Papa dead—

DORINA. And what else could it have been? Love? Could you ever have been in love with a monster like that?

THE LEADING ACTRESS. No!—out of gratitude—

TOTINA. For what?

THE LEADING ACTRESS. For having *believed*—when no one else did—with all the scandal that was going about—

TOTINA. So people could see that at least one of us still could get married?

DORINA. A big deal, to marry *him!*

THE CHARACTER ACTRESS. What did you gain after you married him? Now—now—you'll see.

NENE. (*Returning with a make-up box, a mirror, a towel, the skirt and coat.*) Here's everything. I couldn't find—

THE CHARACTER ACTRESS. Give the box to me. (*She opens the box and begins to do* MOMMINA'S [THE LEADING ACTRESS'S] *make-up.*) Hold up your face. Oh, my child, my child. If you only knew how they talk in town; how they still say, just the way they do of a girl who's dead: "What a pretty girl she was! and what a big heart she had!"—Gone, now—just like this—there,—like this —like this—the face of one who no longer breathes air nor any longer sees the sun—

TOTINA. And the bags under the eyes, the bags under the eyes now.

THE CHARACTER ACTRESS. Yes, there—like this!

DORINA. Not too much!

NENE. What are you saying? On the contrary, a lot, a lot—

TOTINA. The eyes of one who'll die of a broken heart—

NENE. And at the temples, the hair—

THE CHARACTER ACTRESS. Yes, yes—

DORINA. Not white! Not white!

NENE. No, not white—

THE LEADING ACTRESS. My dearest Dorina—

TOTINA. There—fine—like this—at barely thirty years old—

THE CHARACTER ACTRESS. —dusty with age—

THE LEADING ACTRESS. He will no longer even want me to comb my hair—

THE CHARACTER ACTRESS. (*Ruffling her* DAUGHTER's *hair*.) Then wait a minute, like this—like this—

NENE. (*Bringing her the mirror*.) Now take a look at yourself.

THE LEADING ACTRESS. (*Immediately pushing the mirror away with both hands*.) No! He's had all the mirrors in the house taken away. But I still can see myself, though. You know where? In the window panes, like a ghost, or all deformed in the quivering water of a washtub. I stand there stunned, looking.

THE CHARACTER ACTRESS. Wait, her mouth! Her mouth!

THE LEADING ACTRESS. Yes—paint all the red out. I no longer have blood in my veins.

TOTINA. And the wrinkles, the wrinkles at the corners of her mouth—

THE LEADING ACTRESS. Even at thirty, I have lost some of my teeth.

DORINA. (*In an outburst of emotion, embracing her*.) No, no, my sweet Mommina, no, no.

NENE. (*Almost angrily, she too caught up by emotion and pushing* DORINA *away*.) Now her dress—her dress. Let us change her dress—

THE CHARACTER ACTRESS. No. Put the skirt and jacket on over the dress.

TOTINA. Wonderful—she'll look awkward that way.

THE CHARACTER ACTRESS. And her shoulders must be stooped just the way mine are, an old woman's—

DORINA. Trying to get your breath, you go around the house—

THE LEADING ACTRESS. Stunned with grief—

THE CHARACTER ACTRESS. Dragging your feet—

NENE. A walking corpse—

(*Each one, as she says her last line, withdraws into the*

darkness at the Right. THE LEADING ACTRESS, *left alone between the three bare walls of her prison— put up in the dark during the make-up scene— presses her forehead first against the wall at the Right, and then against the one in back, then against the one at the Left. At the touch of her forehead a blinding light from overhead makes the walls visible for a moment, and then they disappear again into darkness.)*

MOMMINA (THE LEADING ACTRESS.) (*In a dismal tone that deepens in intensity as she speaks, knocking her head against the three walls like a crazed animal in a cage.*) This is wall—this is wall—this is wall— (*She goes and sits on the chair with the look of one who is insane. After she has sat there a moment there rises out of the darkness at the Right, where the mother and sisters have withdrawn, a voice, the voice of the mother,* SIGNORA IGNAZIA, *who speaks as if she were reading a story from a book.*)

SIGNORA IGNAZIA. —She was imprisoned in the highest house in town. The doors were locked and all the windows locked, both casements and shutters—only one window, and that very small, was open on the faraway countryside and the faraway sea. Of the town, high on the hill, she saw only rooftops and steeples—roofs, roofs, dripping roofs, dripping here a little more, here a little less, the gutters of many filled up—roof tiles, nothing but roof tiles. Only in the evening could she appear at that window and take some air.

(*In the wall at the rear a little window is lit up, as veiled and faraway, through which shines the soft glimmer of moonlight.*)

NENE. (*From the darkness, softly, happily, with a childlke wonder, while far, far away is heard a feeble*

sound of a gentle serenade.) Oh, the window. Look, it's really a window—
DORINA. Sssshhhh.

(*The* PRISONER *has remained immobile. The* MOTHER *again begins to speak, and always it is as though she were reading.*)

SIGNORA IGNAZIA. —All those rooftops, like so many black dice, used to swim before her feverish eyes in the dusky light the street lamps used to cast in the narrow winding streets of the town. In the heavy silence of nearer alleys she used to hear sounds of echoing footsteps, the voice of some woman who perhaps was waiting as she herself was waiting, or the howling of a dog, or—more painful yet to hear—the sound of the bell in the nearby church, tolling the hour. But why does the clock keep counting the minutes? For whom does it toll the hour? Everything is dead.

(*After a moment five strokes of a BELL are heard, muffled and faraway. It is the clock in the church.* RICO VERRI *appears, sombre and serious. He has just returned home. He still has his hat on his head. The collar of his overcoat is turned up. There is a scarf around his neck. He looks at his wife still sitting motionless in the chair. Then suspiciously he glances at the window.*)

VERRI. What have you been doing?
MOMMINA. Nothing! I was waiting for you.
VERRI. Were you at the window?
MOMMINA. No.
VERRI. You know you're there every evening.
MOMMINA. Not this evening.
VERRI. (*After throwing his coat, his hat, and his scarf on the other big chair.*) Don't you ever get tired of thinking?
MOMMINA. I never think.
VERRI. Are the children in bed?

MOMMINA. Where else would they be at this hour?

VERRI. I ask the question only to remind you of the single thought you ought to have—of them.

MOMMINA. I've thought of them all day long.

VERRI. And what are you thinking of now?

MOMMINA. (*Understanding now why he keeps returning with such insistence to this question, first stares at him scornfully and then, taking up again her pose of motionless apathy, replies.*) Of throwing myself in bed—dead tired—

VERRI. You're lying. I want to know what you're thinking about. What have you been thinking about all the time you've been waiting for me to come? (*An expectant pause, during which she does not answer.*) You won't answer me? You don't dare tell me! (*Another pause.*) So you admit it?

MOMMINA. Admit what?

VERRI. That you're thinking things you don't dare tell me.

MOMMINA. I've told you what I've been thinking of. Going to sleep.

VERRI. Of going to sleep? With those eyes and that voice—? You mean—to *dream!*

MOMMINA. I never dream.

VERRI. That's not true. Everyone dreams. It's not possible to sleep and not to dream.

MOMMINA. I never dream.

VERRI. You're lying, I tell you. It's not possible.

MOMMINA. All right, then. I dream. Have it your way.

VERRI. So you dream, then, do you? You dream. You dream, and you get back at me. You think, and you get back at me. What is it you dream about? Tell me what it is you dream about.

MOMMINA. I don't know.

VERRI. What do you mean you don't know?

MOMMINA. I don't know. It's you who said I dream. I'm so tired at night, my body's so heavy, I'm hardly in bed before I fall asleep, like lead. I no longer know what dreaming means. If I dream and, awakening, no longer recall what it was I dreamt, it's the same as if I'd never dreamt at all. It's perhaps a way God has of helping me.

VERRI. God? *God* helps you?

MOMMINA. Helps me endure a life that would be all the more hideous if for a while dreams had made me think I was leading some other life and then I had to open my eyes on this life again. You know that perfectly well. You know it. What do you want from me? You wish I were dead. Dead. That I no longer thought; that I no longer dreamed. And yet—and yet—to think implies an act of will, but dreaming—if one could dream—would not be an act of will but merely sleeping, and *how* could you forbid me that?

VERRI. (*Agitated, flying into a rage like a beast in a cage.*) That's it! that's it! that's it! I lock the doors, I lock the windows; I put bars up, and grills; but what good does it do me if right here in this prison I'm still betrayed? Here inside you, *inside* you, in this dead body —alive—still alive—betrayal—if you think, if you dream, if you remember. You're standing here before me. You're looking at me. Can I knock open your skull and look inside and find out what it is you're thinking? I ask you what you're thinking, and you say "nothing," and all the while you're thinking, dreaming, remembering, right before my very eyes, *looking at me* while deep down inside you may be remembering *someone else.* How can I find out who it is? How can I see who it is?

MOMMINA. But what do you think there is left inside me, if now I'm no longer anything? Don't you see me standing here? Not even yet another being. No longer anything. I'm burned up. An ash, a mere ash. What can you expect me to remember?

VERRI. Don't talk that way! Don't talk that way! You know you only make it all the worse when you talk that way!

MOMMINA. All right. I won't. Be calm.

VERRI. Even if you went blind, all the things your eyes had already seen, memories, memories you have fixed in your eyes, would be in your mind. And if I tore your lips

off, those lips that have kissed other men's lips, inside
you'd still keep experiencing the pleasure, the pleasure,
the very taste of those other kisses, remembering them
till you died from the pleasure of it. You can't deny it.
If you deny it, you're lying. You can't do anything but
cry, scared of all I suffer on account of you, living with
you, of all the evil you've done me, all your mother and
your sisters taught you. You can't deny it. You've done
them. You've done them, all those horrible things, and
you know how I suffer because of them, suffer to the
point I think I'm going stark mad. It isn't my fault. The
only sign of madness I've ever shown was my madness
in marrying you.

MOMMINA. Madness, yes, madness—you knew yourself
and what you were like. You should never have done it—

VERRI. What *I* was like? Is that what you're saying?
What *I* was like, you say? Knowing what *you* were like,
you *should* say—the kind of life you were leading there,
with your mother and your sisters!

MOMMINA. Yes, yes. That, too. That, too. But don't
forget that you were perfectly aware that I did not ap-
prove of the way they lived—

VERRI. But you lived that way, too—

MOMMINA. Because I had to. I was there—

VERRI. And only when you met me, did you stop ap-
proving of it—

MOMMINA. No. Even before that, even before that.
Anyhow, it's true that in those days you yourself believed
I was superior to the others—I don't say this for my own
sake, to accuse the others and excuse myself, no, I say it
for your sake. So you'll have pity not for me, not for me,
if you're happier in *not* doing so, or rather in showing
others you have none—*be* hard on me, *be* hard on me, but
at least take pity on yourself and remember you *did* believe in me once, that even there in the midst of the life
you despise, you believed you could love me—

VERRI. Enough to marry you! Of course I believed you
were better than the others, but what does that do? How
does that excuse what I did? If I remember I loved you,

that I could love you even there, leading the kind of life you were leading—what good does that do me?

MOMMINA. But don't you see? Recognizing that there was at least something in me that partly excuses the madness you committed in marrying me. There. I'll say it for you.

VERRI. Doesn't that make it all the worse? Do I, with that, cancel out the life you led before I fell in love with you? To have married you because you were better than the others doesn't excuse anything. It only makes it all the worse—since the better you were, all the more hideous, all the more hideous becomes the sinfulness of the life you had led. I've not lifted you up out of it—you've sucked me down into it with you, dragging me down and locking me up here in this prison of yours, to expiate with you all this, as though I'd committed it all myself. Feeling myself eaten alive by it but kept alive by everything I know about your mother and your sisters.

MOMMINA. I no longer know anything about them.

NENE. (*Rising up out of the dark.*) How meanly he is talking about us now.

VERRI. (*Hideously yelling.*) Shut up, you! You're not here!

SIGNORA IGNAZIA. (*Coming to the wall out of the darkness.*) Beast, beast! You've got her there between your teeth, in that cage, and you're ripping her to pieces!

VERRI. (*Touching the walls two times with his hands and, two times at his touch, making the walls visible.*) This is wall! This is wall! *You are not here!*

TOTINA. (*Also coming forward toward the wall with the* OTHERS, *aggressively.*) And you take advantage of it, monster, by telling her filthy lies about us.

DORINA. We were starving, Mommina.

NENE. We'd touched bottom.

VERRI. And how did you get up again?

SIGNORA IGNAZIA. Scoundrel. You dare throw that in our faces while all the time you're slowly *murdering* our Mommina with your cruelty?

NENE. We have an enjoyable life.

VERRI. You sold yourselves. You're dishonored.

TOTINA. And the honor you've kept for her, how do you make up to her for that?

DORINA. Mama's getting along fine now, Mommina. Just see how well she looks. How she dresses! What a gorgeous fur coat she has now!

SIGNORA IGNAZIA. Thanks to Totina. She's become a great singer.

DORINA. Totina La Croce.

NENE. All the theatres are clamoring for her.

SIGNORA IGNAZIA. Parties! One triumph after another!

VERRI. Dishonor!

NENE. I'm all for it, if honor is what you're giving to your wife.

MOMMINA. (*Suddenly, with an impulse of affection and pity for her* HUSBAND, *who has his face in his hands, and seems depressed.*) No, no, I'm not saying that. I'm not saying that. I'm complaining of nothing—

VERRI. They want to condemn me—

MOMMINA. No, no, I understand why you have to shout, to release the torment pent up inside you. You cannot help it.

VERRI. But it's they who keep me in torment. If you only knew the scandals they keep causing. Everyone talks about them Think how I feel. The success they've had has made them let go completely. They're more shameless than ever.

MOMMINA. Dorina, too?

VERRI. All of them. Even Dorina. But most of all, Nene. The little whore—(MOMMINA *covers her face.*)— yes, yes, even in public.

MOMMINA. And Totina has begun to sing?

VERRI. Yes, in theatres—in country towns, of course, where scandals are all the worse, with that mother and those sisters—

MOMMINA. She takes them all with her?

VERRI. All of them. One continuous party— What's the matter? Does it get you excited thinking about it?

MOMMINA. No—it's just that I am learning of all this for the first time. I knew nothing about it before—

VERRI. And you feel yourself all stirred up inside? The theatre, eh? *You* used to sing, didn't you? With that beautiful voice of yours. The most beautiful voice of all was yours. Just think what a different sort of life it would have been for you. To be singing in a big theatre. That was your passion, to sing. Lights, glitter, publicity—

MOMMINA. But, no—

VERRI. Don't say no. You're standing there thinking about it right now.

MOMMINA. I tell you no.

VERRI. What do you mean *no?* If you'd just stuck with them and kept away from me—what a different life you'd have had—instead of this—

MOMMINA. But it's you who are making me think about it. How do you expect me to think any more about anything, when I'm what I am now?

VERRI. You've got that pain again?

MOMMINA. My heart's in my throat—

VERRI. That's it! The pain is showing up again—

MOMMINA. You want to kill me!

VERRI. I? Your sisters, what you were once, your past —that's what's churning up your insides and making your heart jump up in your throat!

MOMMINA. (*Panting, her hands on her chest.*) Please— please—I beg you. I can't get my breath any more—

VERRI. But you see it's true, you see, it's true what I'm telling you.

MOMMINA. Have pity on me—

VERRI. The girl you were—those same thoughts, those same feelings—you thought they were all gone, done with, put out? It isn't true. The merest reminder—and there they all are again, come to life again inside you—

MOMMINA. It's you who remind me of them—

VERRI. No, anything reminds you of them. They're always there, alive, inside you. You don't know it but they're there, beyond anything you know about. You always have inside you the whole life you've lived. All you need is a word, a sound, nothing at all—the smallest sensation. Take me. All I have to do is smell sage and I'm in the country. It's August and I'm a little boy of eight again, behind the gardener's house, in the shade of an old olive tree, afraid of a big blue hornet; miserable because it's buzzing so greedily inside a white flower. I still see that flower trembling on its stalk at being raped by the terrible greed of that hornet that scares me so. And I have it here still, here in my loins, that same fear, I have it right here! Let's just imagine you, and all that fine life you used to lead, and all the things that used to happen between you girls and all those young men who came to the house, shut up alone in this or that room. Don't deny it! I've seen—things. That Nene. One time with Sarelli. They thought they were alone and they'd left the door ajar. I could see them. Nene pretended to go off toward the other room, in the back—there were green curtains there— She went out but came right back, between the green curtains. She'd uncovered her little breasts, pulling down her pink silk slip—and with one hand she was pretending to offer her breast and then right away with the same hand was hiding it. I saw it myself. Beautiful little breasts, you know. Each one just the size you could cup whole in your hand—license to do what one pleases. Before I came to your house—you with Pomarici. Yes, I knew all about it. But before Pomarici— yes, who knows how many others you were with? For years that same life; the house wide open to anyone who came along— (*He stands over her trembling.*) You, certain things—certain things—that you did *first* with me— if up till then you really, as you said, didn't know about them—you couldn't have known how to do them with me—

MOMMINA. No, no, I swear it. Never, never, before I met you—

VERRI. But hugs—embraces—with that Pomarici, yes, —his arms, his arms, didn't they hug you like this? Like this?

MOMMINA. Ahi—you're hurting me.

VERRI. You liked that didn't you? Didn't you? Around your waist, around your waist, like this? Like this?

MOMMINA. Please, please, let go, I'm dying.

VERRI. (*Furiously grabbing her with one hand by the nape of the neck.*) And your mouth, your mouth? How did he kiss your mouth? Like this? Like this? (*And he kisses her, and bites her, and breaks out into loud laughter, and pulls her hair as though crazed.* MOMMINA, *trying to get free, screams desperately.*)

MOMMINA. Help! Help!

(*In their long nightgowns,* THE TWO LITTLE CHILDREN, *girls, terrified by the noises, run in and cling to their mother.* VERRI *runs out of the room, grabbing from the chair only his hat.*)

VERRI. (*Yelling.*) I'm going crazy! I'm going crazy! I'm going crazy!

MOMMINA. (*Protecting herself and making a shield of her body for* THE TWO CHILDREN.) Get out of here, get out, get out, monster! Leave me alone with my babies— (*She sinks down exhausted on the chair.* THE TWO CHILDREN *are beside her, and she holds them tightly, embracing them, one on one side and one on the other.*) My little ones, my little ones, the things you've had to see! Locked up here with me—with your waxen faces and your great big eyes wide open with fear. He's gone now. He's gone now. Don't tremble any more like this. You can stay here with me a little while. Here with me. Are you sure you aren't cold? The window's closed. It's so late already. You're always glued to the window there, like two little beggars begging for—a glimpse of the world. Always counting the white sails of the sloops at sea, aren't you? And the little cottages scattered across the fields where you've never been. And you're always asking me what it's like, the sea—and the fields. Oh, children, children, what a life you've had. Worse than mine. But at least you don't know it. And your mother's so sick—so sick here, in her heart. It beats so hard, here in her breast, it's like a gallop, like the gallop of a runaway horse. Here, here, give me your little hands—feel it, feel it! May God not make him pay for it—for your sakes, children. But he'll make martyrs out of you, because he can't help it. It's his nature. He made himself a martyr, too—but you're innocent. You are innocent—

(*She presses the little hands of* THE TWO CHILDREN *to her checks and remains like this. From the Right, at the wall, emerging from the darkness like conspirators, the mother,* SIGNORA IGNAZIA, *and* THE DAUGHTERS *approach her, gorgeously dressed and making a colorful scene. They are, it should be noted, effectively lit from overhead.*)

SIGNORA IGNAZIA. (*Softly calling.*) Mommina—Mommina—

MOMMINA. Who is it?

DORINA. It's us, Mommina.

NENE. We're here. All of us.

MOMMINA. Here? Where?

TOTINA. Here. In the town. I've come to sing.

MOMMINA. Totina—you? to sing here?

NENE. Yes, in the theatre here.

MOMMINA. Oh God, here? And when? When?

NENE. This evening. This very evening.

SIGNORA IGNAZIA. My dears, leave something for me to say. Listen, Mommina, look—what was it I wanted to say? Oh, yes. Look, you want proof of it? Your husband left his coat over there, there on that chair—

MOMMINA. (*Turning to look.*) Yes, he did.

SIGNORA IGNAZIA. Look in one of the pockets of the coat and see what you find there. (*Softly to the girls.*) We must help her get into her big scene now. We're near the end of the performance.

MOMMINA. (*Getting up and going to search feverishly in the pockets of the coat.*) What is it I'm looking for? What is it I'm looking for?

NENE. (*Softly to* SIGNORA IGNAZIA.) Will you answer her?

SIGNORA IGNAZIA. No, no, you— What a fuss!

NENE. (*Loudly to* MOMMINA.) It's a handbill—you know, a little yellow sheet, the kind they pass out in cafes, in country towns—

SIGNORA IGNAZIA. There you'll find Totina's name, printed in large letters—the name of the prima donna.

(*They vanish.*)

MOMMINA. (*Finding it.*) Here it is! Here it is! (*She opens it and reads.*) *Il Trovatore. Il Trovatore.* Lenora— soprano—Totina La Croce—this evening. Your aunt, children, your aunt. It's your aunt who's singing Lenora. And your grandmother and your other aunts are all here, are *here!* You don't know them. You've never seen them—nor have I, for many years. They're here. (*Thinking of her husband's anger.*) Ah, it was all because of this—they here in town, Totina singing in the theatre here. There is a theatre here, then? I didn't even know there was one. Aunt Totina. Then it's true. Perhaps, with study, her voice— Surely, if she can sing in public— But, my children, my poor little children, you don't even know what a theatre is—a theatre, a theatre—now I shall tell you what a theatre is. Tonight your Aunt Totina is singing in one. And oh how beautiful she'll be as Lenora— (*She tries to sing.*)

> "Tacea la notte placida
> e bella in ciel sereno
> la luna il viso argenteo
> mostrava lieto e pieno—"

You see. I too can sing. Yes, yes. I too can sing. I used to sing all the time once. Yes, I did. I know all of *Trovatore* by heart. And I'm going to sing it for you now. I'll make the theatre for you first—you who've never seen one, my poor little chicks, shut up in your prison here with your mummy. Sit down, sit down here in front of me, right here on your little chairs. I'll make a theatre for you. First I'll tell you what it's like. (*She sits before the two stunned* CHILDREN. *She herself is trembling all over, and from moment to moment she will become increasingly excited until finally her heart will fail her and she will suddenly fall dead on the floor.*) A hall, a big, big hall, with many rows of boxes all around; five, six rows, full of beautiful women, with feathers and jewels and fans and flowers. And the gentlemen all in tails, with little pearls for buttons on their shirts. And with white ties. And so many, many people everywhere, even below, in red plush chairs, in the orchestra. A sea of heads. And lights, lights everywhere. A great chandelier in the center that hangs down as though it were hanging down from heaven itself, and all covered with glittering crystals. Oh, how dazzling it is. It makes you dizzy. You can't imagine how dazzling the light is and how dizzy it makes you— Noise and movement—the ladies are all talking with elegant gentlemen, greeting each other from one box to the next; some who take their places below in the orchestra; others who are looking with their glasses—like the ones of mother-of-pearl that I've made you look at the fields with—yes, those—I used to carry them—yes, your own mother used to carry them—when she went to the theatre and used them to look around, ah, yes, some time ago. All of a sudden the lights go down. Only the little green lights on the desks of the orchestra—in front of the seats —there below the curtain—stay lit. The players are already in their places—oh, so many of them—and they're all tuning up. And the curtains are like window curtains, but large, and heavy, all red velvet splattered with gold, magnificent things really. When they open—for the conductor's come out with his baton to lead the players—the opera begins. And you see the stage now. There's a forest, or a square, or a palace. And Aunt Totina's coming out and singing with the others, and the orchestra is playing —that's the theatre— But I once, I once had the more beautiful voice, not your Aunt Totina. I, I had a very much more beautiful voice. I had a voice that made everyone say I should sing opera. I. Your own mother. In-

stead it's your Aunt Totina who's done it. Ah, she had the courage to do it. The curtain's opening now. Listen. They draw it back from both sides. Once it's open you see on the stage a hall in a great palace, and armed men that march up and down in the rear. And many knights, including a certain Ferrando. They're all waiting for their captain, the Conte di Luna. They're dressed up in a funny old-fashioned way, with velvet coats and plumed hats and swords and padded legs. It's night. They're tired of waiting for the count who, in love with a great lady in the Spanish court—her name is Lenora—is jealous of her and stays hidden under her balcony to spy on her. In the gardens of the palace. He knows that every night a trovatore, a troubadour, a man who is both a singer and a knight, comes and sings her this song. (*She sings.*)
        "Deserto sulla terra—"
(*She interrupts herself for a moment to say, almost to herself.*) Oh God, my heart— (*And immediately begins to sing again, but with effort, struggling with the pain caused, of course, by the excitement of hearing herself sing again.*)
        "Col rio destino in guerra
        é sola speme un cor—"
            (*Sung three times and then.*)
        "un cor—al Trovator—"
I can't sing any more—I—I—can't get my breath—the heart—my heart hurts so—I haven't sung for a great many years—but perhaps little by little, my breath, my voice, will come back to me— You must understand that this troubadour is a brother of the Conte di Luna—yes, but the count, of course, does not know this, and the troubadour himself does not know it, either—for he was kidnapped by a gypsy when he was a little baby. It's a terrible story you're about to hear. You'll see this gypsy in the second act. Her name is Azucena. Yes, that was my part, that was my part, the role of Azucena. She stole the baby, this Azucena, to revenge her mother's death, her mother, who was innocently burned alive by the father of the Conte di Luna. Gypsies are vagabonds that

tell your fortune and read the future, and they still exist. They're still said to kidnap children, so much so that mama is very careful about them. But this Azucena steals the son of the count, as I've just told you, to revenge the death of her own mother, and she plans to give him the very death her own mother suffered. And she gets the fire going big. But in the fury of her revenge, half-crazed, she grabs up her own child, her own little boy, instead of the count's and throws *him* on the fire. You understand? "Il figlio mio—il figlio mio—" I can't—I can't sing it for you. You don't know, my children, what this evening means to me, and especially *Trovatore*—this song of the gypsy—it's the one I was singing one night, with everyone around me— (*She sings, crying at the same time.*)

> "Chi del gitano la vita abbella?
> La zingarella!"

My father that night, my father—your grandfather—was brought back home all covered with blood—and he had with him a kind of gypsy that night—and that night, that very night, children, my fate—my fate was sealed—my fate— (*She gets up desperately and sings with all her strength.*)

> "Ah che la morte ognora
> é tarda nel venir
> a chi desia
> a chi desia morir!
> Addio,
> addio, Lenora, addio—"

(*She suddenly collapses on the floor, dead.* THE TWO CHILDREN, *more bewildered than ever, have no inkling of what has happened. They think it is still the opera that their mother is doing for them. And they sit there motionless in their little chairs, waiting. The silence and the immobility become unbearable. Finally, in the darkness, from the rear at the Left, come the anxious voices of* RICO VERRI, *of* SIGNORA IGNAZIA, *of* TOTINA, DORINA, *and* NENE.)

VERRI. She was singing. Did you hear it? It was *her* voice—

SIGNORA IGNAZIA. Yes. A bird in a cage!

TOTINA. Mommina! Mommina!

DORINA. It's us—we're here with him. He's admitted he was wrong—

NENE. It was Totina's triumph that did it—he understood—the town went delirious— (*She starts to say "delirious" but she breaks off in the middle, terrified like the others at the sight of the lifeless body there on the floor before them and of* THE TWO CHILDREN *that are still waiting, motionless.*)

VERRI. What's the matter?

SIGNORA IGNAZIA. Dead?

DORINA. She was playing theatre for the children!

TOTINA. Mommina—

NENE. Mommina—

(*They stand in fixed poses. From the door into the hall of the theatre, running down the aisle straight onto the stage,* DR. HINKFUSS *enthusiastically rushes to them.*)

DR. HINKFUSS. Magnificent! A truly magnificent scene! You did it just as I told you to. *This* is not in the story at all.

SIGNORA IGNAZIA. (*As* THE CHARACTER ACTRESS). He's here again!

THE CHARACTER ACTOR. (*Appearing from the Left.*) But he was here all the time, hidden over there with the electricians, seeing to all the lighting effects.

NENE. So that explains it—they were beautiful—

TOTINA. I guessed it. When we appeared together— (*She points to the other side of the stage, to the Right, behind the wall.*) that beautiful effect from overhead—

THE CHARACTER ACTRESS. (*Pointing again to* MOMMINA [THE LEADING ACTRESS] *lying on the floor.*) But why don't you get up, Miss ————? She's still lying there—

THE CHARACTER ACTOR. She couldn't really be dead, could she?

(ALL *gently bend down over* THE LEADING ACTRESS.)

THE LEADING ACTOR. (*Calling to her and lifting her up.*) Miss ————
THE CHARACTER ACTRESS. Are you really sick?
NENE. Good God, she's fainted. Let's lift her up.
THE LEADING ACTRESS. (*Getting up herself.*) No—thank you. It really *is* my heart, though. Let me get my breath. Let me get my breath—
THE CHARACTER ACTOR. Of course, of course—if you really want us to *live* our roles, this is what happens. But get this, we aren't here to do this kind of thing. We're here to play written parts, memorized before hand, learned by heart. Don't you think for a minute that every evening each of us is going to get out of his own skin like this—
THE LEADING ACTOR. We need the author.
DR. HINKFUSS. The author, no. Written parts, yes, if we must—just so they can for one moment be endowed with the life we alone can give them and—(*He turns to the audience.*) without a repetition of this evening's errors, for which I must beg—the audience's forgiveness. (*He bows.*)

CURTAIN

TONIGHT WE IMPROVISE

PROPERTY PLOT

ACT ONE

A little scroll—Dr. Hinkfuss

ACT TWO
PROCESSION

4 lit tapers—Choirboys
A little baldachin of skyblue silk with 4 supports—Young
  Girls
1 long staff, flowered at the crook—Joseph
A big wax doll—Mary
1 set of bagpipes—Shepherd
1 flute—Young Shepherd
More bagpipes—Musicians

ACT TWO
THE NIGHT CLUB

1 street lamp
1 bar
A flaming red velvet drapery
About 4 small round tables
About 6 straight chairs
1 long cigar—Sampognetta
2 long horns cut out of a light cardboard menu—The
  Joking Customer

ACT TWO
THE THEATRE

A box set-up
2 benches
3 or 4 chairs

INTERLUDE
IN THE LOBBY

Refreshment stand
Soft drinks
1 bag of chocolates

1 box of caramels
A bench

ACT THREE
SIGNORA IGNAZIA'S HOME

A pretentious sideboard
A candlestick with a candle in it—on sideboard
A box of matches—on sideboard
A cork bottlestopper—on sideboard
4 or 5 brass fingerbowls—on sideboard
A table in the dining room
A red cloth—on the table
A bellshaped lampshade of orange and green—over the table
An armchair
A sofa
A stool
A piano (can be offstage)
A small table (Down Center—to be used for the candlestick later)
A black silk handkerchief—SIGNORA IGNAZIA
A little statue of the Madonna—off rear—NENE
A big hat with a feather—off rear—NENE
A red shawl—off rear—NENE
Make-up for a moustache—POMARICI
A wig—SIGNORA IGNAZIA (as THE CHARACTER ACTRESS)

ACT THREE
TRANSITION AND PRISON SCENE

2 straight back chairs—Off Right—STAGE HANDS and APPOINTED ACTORS
2 small wooden children's chairs—Off Right—STAGE HANDS and APPOINTED ACTORS
A make-up box with appropriate materials inside—Off Right—NENE
A towel—Off Right—NENE
A hand mirror—Off Right—NENE
A skirt for MOMMINA—Off Right—NENE
A coat for MOMMINA—Off Right—NENE
    (costumes used as props)

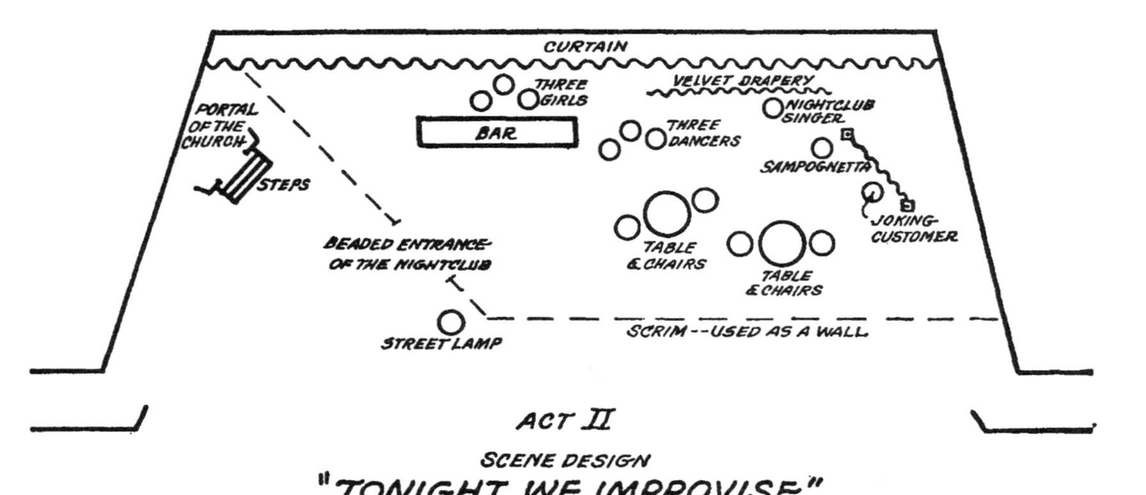

ACT II

SCENE DESIGN

"TONIGHT WE IMPROVISE"

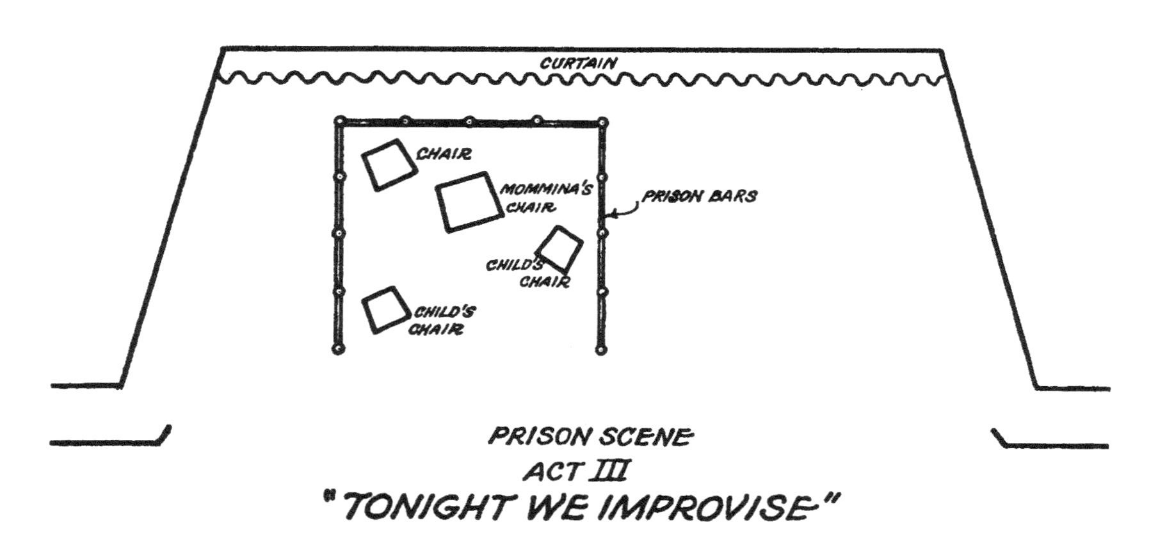

PRISON SCENE
ACT III
"TONIGHT WE IMPROVISE"

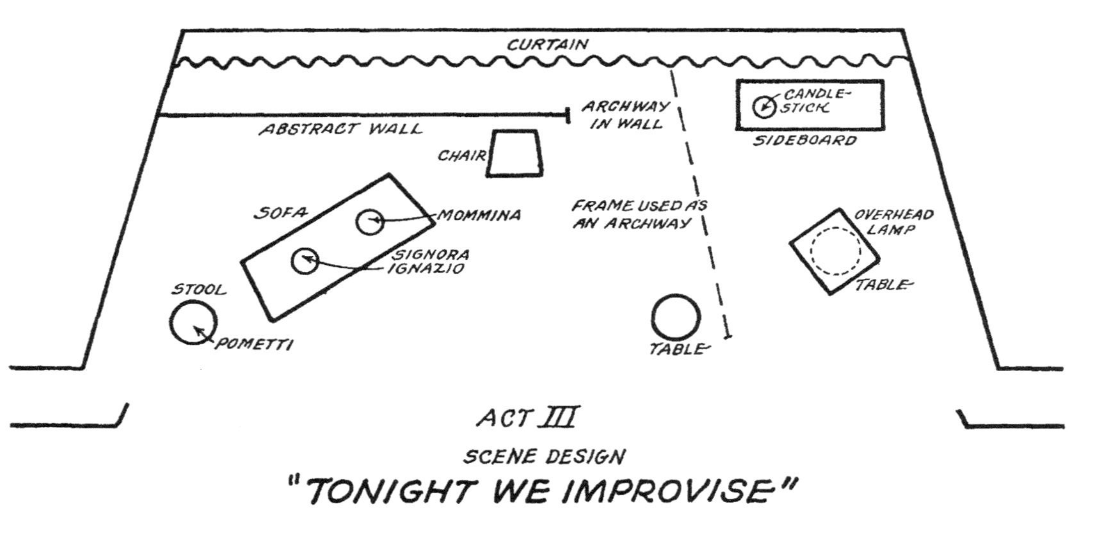

ACT III

SCENE DESIGN

"TONIGHT WE IMPROVISE"

MUSIC USE NOTE

Licensees are solely responsible for obtaining formal written permission from copyright owners to use copyrighted music in the performance of this play and are strongly cautioned to do so. If no such permission is obtained by the licensee, then the licensee must use only original music that the licensee owns and controls. Licensees are solely responsible and liable for all music clearances and shall indemnify the copyright owners of the play(s) and their licensing agent, Samuel French, against any costs, expenses, losses and liabilities arising from the use of music by licensees. Please contact the appropriate music licensing authority in your territory for the rights to any incidental music.

IMPORTANT BILLING AND CREDIT REQUIREMENTS

If you have obtained performance rights to this title, please refer to your licensing agreement for important billing and credit requirements.

www.ingramcontent.com/pod-product-compliance
Lightning Source LLC
Chambersburg PA
CBHW070632120726
47909CB00004B/1405